Tales by the World's Great Contemporary Writers Presented Unabridged

All selections in
Short Story International
are reprinted full and
unabridged in the author's
own words. Nothing is
added, subtracted,
condensed or rewritten.

Editor
Sylvia Tankel

Associate Editor
Erik Sandberg-Diment

Contributing Editor
John Harr

Assistant Editors
Mildred Butterworth
Arlene Loveless
Kirsten Hammerle

Art Director
Mort Rubenstein

Drawings by
Charles Walker

Circulation Director
Nat Raboy

Production Director
Ludwig K. Marz

Business Manager
John O'Connor

Publisher
Sam Tankel

Volume 7, Number 36, February 1983
Short Story International (USPS 375-970)
Copyright © by International Cultural
Exchange 1983. Printed in the U.S.A. All
rights reserved. Reproduction in whole or in
part prohibited. Second-class postage paid
at Great Neck, N.Y. 11022 and at additional
mailing offices. **Editorial offices: P.O. Box
405, Great Neck, N.Y. 11022.** Enclose
stamped, self-addressed envelope with
previously published stories submitted for
possible reprinting in *Short Story
International*. Please note *SSI* does not
accept unpublished original manuscripts.
One year (six issues) subscription for U.S.,
U.S. possessions $16, Canada $18 (US),
other countries $21 (US). All institutions add
$2 per annual subscription. Single copy
price $3.45. **For subscriptions and
address changes write to *Short Story
International*. P.O. Box 405, Great Neck,
N.Y. 11022.** *Short Story International* is
published bimonthly by International
Cultural Exchange, 6 Sheffield Road, Great
Neck, N.Y. 11021. Postmaster please send
Form 3579 to P.O. Box 405, Great Neck,
N.Y. 11022.

Note from the Editor

Who doesn't enjoy a good laugh?

In days of yore, a reigning king would command his jester to turn a troubling weight from his mind. It was the wise and talented jester whose play with words would divert the king and brighten a tense or dull assembly.

Today we are fortunate to have gifted writers who use their powerful pens (or word processors) to divert our minds from the gloom of newspaper headlines. Such a talent is E.G. Peacock of England who brings "The Chief Clerk" to this issue.

Another such talent, but with a satiric twist, is Aziz Nesin from Turkey who has appeared in several issues of *Short Story International*. In this issue, his "The Rusty Tin Can in the Treasury" is open to many interpretations.

Desmond O'Grady from Australia is another writer with that magical quality. Try his "Yours Sincerly" (no spelling error on our part).

SSI does not limit itself to laughter. Our authors face up to the many realities in this world. For example, "The Witness Man" by Vincent O'Sullivan of New Zealand focuses on justice and the regard for an aged witness. It is poignant. So too is "I Stand Here Ironing" by Tillie Olsen of the USA. Tillie Olsen has a small body of published work, but it is as polished as a precious jewel.

Each story in *SSI* has its own special magnetism. And what comes through is that humankind has the will to survive...and to make time for a resuscitating bit of laughter. Armageddon is not yet upon us.

Copyrights and acknowledgments

We wish to express deep thanks to the authors, publishers, translators and literary agents for their permission to publish the stories in this issue.

"A Vibration in the Memory" by Maureen Pople first appeared in *Canberra Times*. Copyright Maureen Pople 1977. "Yours Sincerly" from *Valid for All Countries* by Desmond O'Grady. Copyright Desmond O'Grady 1979. "A Sunless Morning" by Li Guangtian from *Chinese Literature*, 1981. Translation by Gladys Yang. "The Chief Clerk" by E.G. Peacock first appeared in *Blackwood's Magazine*, 1980. Reprinted by permission of the author and editor of *Blackwood's Magazine*. "Case History" by E.G. Chipulina, 1983. "The Yellow Line" by S. Komala. Copyright © 1980 S. Komala. "Christmas in Hungary" by Paul-Thomas M. Szabadság first appeared in *Orion*. Reprinted by permission. "The Sunny Side after the Harvest" from *Love in Winter* by Kim Yong Ik. Copyright Kim Yong Ik. "The Changing Tide" by Alias Ali from *Modern Malaysian Stories*, translated by Barclay M. Newman. Published by Dewan Bahasa dan Pustaka Malaysia. Copyright © Alias Ali 1977. "The Waterfall" from *Estimado Yo* by Bruno Schwebel. Copyright © 1979 Editorial Diana. Translation by the author and Joan Brodovsky. "The Witness Man" by Vincent O'Sullivan first appeared in *Landfall*, 1980. Copyright Vincent O'Sullivan 1980. "Tong" from *Waywaya and Other Short Stories from the Philippines* by F. Sionil José. Published by Heinemann Educational Books (Asia) Ltd. Copyright © 1980 F. Sionil José. "The Big Deal" by Rosalind Morton. Copyright © Rosalind Morton 1983. "The Rusty Tin Can in the Treasury" from *Memleketin Birinde* by Aziz Nesin. Translation by Joseph S. Jacobson, 1983. "The Disappearance of Certain Small Communities" by William Doxey first appeared in *Forum*, Vol. 10, No. 1 Reprinted by permission. "I Stand Here Ironing" from *Tell Me A Riddle* by Tillie Olsen. Copyright © 1956 Tillie Olsen. Reprinted by permission of Delacorte Press/Seymour Lawrence. Published in the Bristish Commonwealth by Virago Press, London.

Photo credits: Tillie Olsen by Pete Amos

Table of Contents

"Just the sight of him was enough to ensure that his word was never challenged."

A Vibration in the Memory

BY MAUREEN POPLE

CHILLA spent a lot of time on the banks of Parsons Creek. *Mollocking.*

She'd hear the motorbike first, thrumming across the paddock beside the house. Chilla crouched over the petrol tank and the girl of the day crouched over Chilla. You could say one thing for Chilla, he played fair. Every girl in town who'd passed the age of consent had had the chance to consent to Chilla, and each had taken the ride cheerfully towards a fate much better than death.

Just beyond the fowl run the path swerved to the right and Chilla and girl would lean right over there, and then, in perfect unison, they'd sway upright again. As pretty to watch as a pair of figure skaters.

He always took them to the same spot. They'd dismount and he'd position the bike as carefully as if it were his ailing granma he was taking on a picnic. Now you sit there Gran and look at the view. The girl would prance about a bit, obviously eager to start gathering rosebuds. Then Chilla would spit over his shoulder, and together they would disappear behind the curtain of willow fronds.

She, too, had gathered some rosebuds in her day and God knows the girls can take care of themselves now. But it troubled her, because of Chilla. Chilla was no good.

Each afternoon, when the hooter from the mill had whined, the young lads of the town would gather on the street outside the general store. An old hitching rail stood there. No horse had been seen in town for some years, but the rail had become the rallying point for this daily ritual. As the stores and the offices closed, the girls would emerge, and saunter past the general store. And the hitching rail. Chattering with brilliant vivacity, listening with rapt interest, flicking glances at their gay reflections in the shop windows, completely unaware of the boys' presence.

And the young men's voices would become a little louder, and deeper, as they jostled each other about in the dust of the roadside. They appeared not to notice the girls going by. But every now and then one of them would leave the group and, hands in pockets, set off down the street. A girl would suddenly lose interest in her friends' conversation and walk a little slower. And so they paired off, the width of the pavement between them at first, and not speaking at all until they were well out of earshot of the group by the hitching rail.

Chilla bestrode this little world like a colossus, in that he outdid all the other youths in uncouthness. The owner of the general store called him a *mug lair* (but never out loud!) and wished he would move along (but never suggested it!). Because Chilla was tough. If there had been a chapter of Hells Angels in Parsons Creek, Chilla would doubtless have been its leader. Given the bicycle chain of office as it were. But there were few bikes in town, and Chilla needed no gang to support him. Just the sight of him was enough to ensure that his word was never challenged. His hair was black and greasy. His face was brown and greasy, with expressions ranging from dumb insolence to belligerent insolence. He had no other expression. He spat a lot, a gambit frequently employed by the young men of the town to conceal a lack of social graces. One presumed that he could speak, but he was seldom caught in the act. God only knew how he enticed those girls onto his pillion. They answered a call of the wild inaudible to the rest of the town.

Most of the young men worked at the sawmill, a few helped run a family farm. Those who worked in the town were never counted in the group around the hitching rail. They had opportunities to arrange their love life during office hours. One of the envied perquisites of the while collar worker.

Chilla did no regular work, but was in great demand as an itinerant laborer. In the season he did a spot of wheat lumping at the railway, shouldering the heavy bags from the farmers' lorries onto the railway trucks. He was available for bulldozing or tractor work when the need arose. Chilla's need that is. He was slave to no man and worked only when the fancy took him. Or when the bike needed repairs.

When Chilla presided at the hitching rail, his dress was bizarre and distinctive, at least for Parsons Creek. Black pants, tight and shiny; leather jacket, worn summer and winter, autumn and spring, along with scuffed and vicious flying boots. All the better to kick you with my dear.

Thus the older folk of the town saw Chilla, and that was why the woman at the farm would turn away after the bike had passed, and tighten her lips and shake her head.

One day in summer there was extra work to be done at the farm, and help for a day was needed. Her husband went to town in the old utility and came back to report that tomorrow was the day and he'd got a good worker for the job.

"It's that young Charlie Bates—one they call Chilla."

"Why him?"

"Only one I could get, love. They say he's a good worker."

"Well I don't want him inside this house, that's all. Riffraff, that's what he is."

He arrived on time the next day, on his motorbike. It was strange to see it veer left instead of right towards the creek, and strange also to see Chilla in his working clothes. She watched from the veranda as he parked the bike with his customary solicitude beneath the old pepper tree. He looked just like a normal young lad, she thought.

Khaki shorts and a clean working shirt. But the belligerent face reassured her. He was riffraff alright. She turned away, calling to her husband.

"He's here. I've packed your lunch."

They drove off together in the utility, along the fence of the home paddock, past the willows of the creek, and out of sight. She was glad she'd packed them food for lunch, gave her a chance to get a few extra things done around the house and a nice sit on the veranda when the work was done.

Not much to see though. The cattle down by the creek were struck motionless by the heat and the only moving things in sight were the crows, wheeling, dipping, mournful, raucous.

She wondered how her husband was getting on with that strange boy, and wished again that someone more conventional had been available. He looked strong enough for the work. Strong enough to beat you up and rob you—that's how strong he looked—and thank God here was the truck now, bouncing along the track towards the house.

Chilla climbed down and stood beside it while her husband came across to the wicket gate.

"I've told Charlie he can eat with us Mum, that OK?"

She nodded grudgingly, hating him for his easy-going friendliness. She'd said she didn't want that boy inside her house and now she'd have to feed him. Leaving the rocker to squeak the protests that she dared not voice herself, she went into the hot kitchen to prepare the meal.

"Be ready in half an hour," she muttered mutinously over her shoulder. She roused the embers in the old fuel stove and tied on her gingham apron. Her husband lumbered across to the bathroom to wash.

Chilla's motorbike roared into life.

"Where's he off to then?"

"Dunno. I said we'd have a beer. Musta gone to have one at the pub. He'll be back."

He came into the kitchen, face red and shining with the scrubbing, hair wet and rimy with dried soap.

"Funny chap. Don't talk much. Good worker though. Like a beer?"

"No thank you." He could keep his beer. Inviting people like that to eat with you. "He won't be back. Gone to pick up a girl friend. That's what he's done."

She banged the old saucepans onto the black hob. I'd love a beer, a nice cold beer, she thought. I'll have one if he offers again. But he wouldn't offer, she knew, and she wouldn't ask for one. Not if she was dying of thirst she wouldn't. He was very quick to invite young hoodlums into the house, but his wife, *she* could faint dead away from the heat in this kitchen and he wouldn't notice.

Unaware of the ominous cold war that was raging about him, the husband sat drinking his beer and reading the local paper.

"Says here the new silo'll open this year."

"Meal's ready."

"Wait a bit longer."

"Did he *say* he wanted to eat here?"

"Well he grunted, sounded like he wanted to."

So the meal would be ruined. She hated serving an overcooked meal. Already the gravy was getting a skin on it. She sat at the table, plucking an old stain from her apron. And there was the sound of the motorbike, not fading off to the creek, but coming right up to the house again.

"Well, at last. He's here. Meal's ruined."

The bike stopped. Heavy footsteps beat across the veranda and the screen door opened.

Chilla stood framed in the doorway. Black tight shiny pants, scuffed flying boots, leather jacket. And his hair, glistening with brilliantine, filled the room with the odor of exotic and decadent blossoms.

Slowly the woman rose to her feet.

"Sit down there, Charlie. Meal's not quite ready yet. Be back in a minute."

Into the bedroom, fumbling with the knot of her apron as she went. Kicked off her bunioned slippers and groped under the bed for her town shoes. The Christmas box of talc stood on her dressing table. She puffed some over her shiny nose, fluffed up her hair, and *swanned* back into the kitchen.

"Think I will have that beer now Ted, then I'll dish up your meal."

He was riffraff all right, uncouth, morose, and still to be feared. But she realized, with the music of soft voices in her memory, that he had paid her the finest compliment he knew.

Chilla was visiting a lady, so he'd gone home to change into his *mollocking suit.*

While recuperating after an illness in 1976, Maureen Pople was nudged into writing short stories. Since then she has been collecting prizes for her writings. She was awarded first prize in the Short Story of the Year (Canberra Times) *1976, the Henry Lawson Award for Prose 1978, the Melbourne Sun Short Story Festival 1978, and the Maryborough Festival Award 1978. Her story "One Day in the Life of Mrs. Riley" appeared in SSI No. 27. She also writes novels and plays for stage, radio and television. Maureen Pople is married to an engineer; they have two daughters.*

"I had been rigid with righteousness when I had challenged Wallace."

Yours Sincerly

BY DESMOND O'GRADY

"THEY were Jehovah Witnesses," said my wife, between amusement and annoyance, when she came from the door, "warning that you never know when He's coming. Told them I was a Buddhist."

She had an air of "as-if-I-didn't-have-enough-to-do." My daughter wanted to know what Witnesses were. When my wife said they would not allow transfusions even when children are dying, it excited her interest further.

I asked if they had left any pamphlets.

"Who'd want them?" said my wife. On her way to the kitchen she began to answer my daughter's anxious questions. Who'd want them? I would. I could see the slim pamphlets, poorly printed, with the biblical quotes perhaps in red—impelling, incandescent. I imagined the Wintesses as carrot-haired, gawky, afflicted by adolescent acne despite adulthood, eyes glazed with the fervor of a belief which I regarded, momentarily, with nostaligic envy.

Once I too had awaited—no invoked—the Second Coming. I knew the longing of those who expect the Lord to unmask hypocrites, humble the mighty, and separate the just from the unjust.

I had toyed with the idea of of the judgment day for some time before I seized on it like a sword. An old aunt's words, "It's not the dying but the judgment which worries me," had embedded themselves deep; but what I relished was the theatrical end-of-the-world bit, the angels trumpeting the arrival of the Lord in a magnesium-flash of majesty. The end-of-the-world appealed as the last laugh on quotidianity: you could not get too sunk into your part to forget that at any minute the painted scene might be whipped away.

I could not remember who first spoke of the judgment day to us: awareness seemed to be planted like those seeds which sprout only after a scorching fire. It could not have been Father Curtin, at the church which adjoined the school, as he was more likely to talk of second innings than of the Second Coming. It may have been the Brothers, but they were more intent on conveying a version of the beyond inherited from distant Ireland: not leprechauns but stories such as that of a headmaster passing outside third-floor classrooms, on the side of a building with a sheer drop to the ground, fifteen years after his death. Intended to fill us with awe for the prodigies of the holy, it chilled us with the hint that the beyond was a vast Brothers' school. The Irish-beyond counseled caution but the Irish-past nourished a desire for justice even if in terms of comeuppance. Assigned a three-page essay on a topic of my choice, I had turned in a twenty-five page dirge inspired by Ireland's wrongs. But the scorching fire which caused the seeds to sprout was ignited by Brother Whacker Wallace rather than by mulling over the Black and Tans' misdeeds.

Wallace wanted to denounce me to my father on his return from a trip to Sydney. Although my father and I were a pair both physically (slim, long-faced, with crinkly sandy hair) and psychologically (determined, proud), I feared he might believe Wallace's distortions because of his profound respect for the Brothers. But I knew I was justified before heaven. I prayed that the skies split open the Friday my father was to see Wallace, revealing his true colors.

I had been rigid with righteousness when I had challenged Wallace. Beginning of drawing class: as usual, Wallace, boisterous philistine, had asked our art teacher Holditch to hand over for a moment. "You chaps are free, of course, to sketch and etch but if you'd devote five minutes to addressing these envelopes, you'd help bring the faith to those born without it."

Holditch standing aside, smiling as if it hurt, one hand exploring the back of the hair which we swore was a wig. Two strikes against him: a layman and an art teacher. Any layman teaching in a Brothers' school was suspect of a murky background ranging from a lack of proper qualifications to unspeakable practices which would exclude him from the State circuit. Holditch was shaky on several counts. He was a kind of cut-price Beau Brummel, a bachelor who on weekends cruised the bayside suburbs in an old, white MG. He taught meticulously but with a resigned detachment, perhaps because art teaching was considered the refuge of the limp-wristed and art classes as fatuous as our earlier singing or elocution lessons. The Barcarole. Tit Willow...

Although Holditch wilted before Wallace, one true artist set about his work while the remainder of the class happily addressed begging letters. They were not inspired by zeal for the heathens Wallace's brother was converting in the Solomons but by the opportunity to skip drawing and keep on the right side of Whacker.

They were five minutes, usually going on fifteen, which Wallace regularly stole from the art class. A quarter of an hour of badinage between Wallace and the boys as he waived the rule of silence which prevailed in his own classes.

That day, however, the noise gradually decreased until I felt I was drawing isolated on a dais. I fenced out the uncanny silence as I wanted to pin Wallace to his words. Also I enjoyed showing I was different. I was determined to prove it further by not marrying nor drinking nor smoking nor falling into any of the drab compromises which I saw around me.

When I looked up, Wallace was standing close by, hands on hips.

His brushed-back black hair seemed to stand up, his eyes behind his black-rimmed spectacles were owlish, a pallor appeared under his tan. "Well done Corcoran," he said, small-voiced between tight lips, "later you must show me your masterpiece which is so much more important than helping those without the faith."

Finesse, however, was not his forte. The explosion came towards the end of the following geography class during which Wallace had ignored me. A prefect entered to hand him a slip of paper which he read to the class: "Hehir and Corcoran have been selected to play for the first eleven in the match which begins at two tomorrow."

We were the youngest pair to have been selected for the team.

"Don't tell me you want sonsy Corcoran!"

"Could be our best all-rounder," was the answer from the prefect who could not credit blatant antipathy. Perhaps he did not know that Wallace was never among the Brothers who stopped at the school nets to admire my cutting. For all his exuberance, Wallace's sporting activities were confined to handball and strapping.

Then Wallace was away: telling the uncomfortable prefect that I was full of myself, invidious, ungrateful, cynical...There was no stopping him in these tirades but he must have realized he had overstepped the mark. When the bell to end the session sounded, he detained me. He explained that he had been upset not by my refusal to address the envolopes, because he had made it clear it was a free choice, but by my rank ingratitude after all he had done for me, the hardening of heart in one he had believed was unspoiled. He said he would talk to my father about me. I was seething but silent. It worried me that he wanted to see my father. I regretted I could not ask Father Curtin to prevent the meeting, as on a previous occasion when he had unwittingly abetted my truancy.

Curtin was the first person I had met who could match my cricket lore. Somewhere in his presbytery packed with cricket books there must have been volumes also on the theology of Test Matches and the spirituality of spin bowling. He spoke of the game with a rueful love as if it were a paradise from which he was excluded; I never found out whether this was due to his clerical state or excess weight.

I had ferreted out arcane cricket manuals in the public library; I knew that cricket books could be consulted free in several secondhand bookshops; I had a collection of Wisdens. Not only had I read C.B. Turner on the art of bowling, I was writing my own study on left-arm leg-spin bowling.

Curtin told me how disappointed he was that, as he had to give lectures in a distant convent, he could not see the New South Wales side, particularly Bill Alley.

I decided to take his place on the first day and give him a report on his return. The match was played at the Carlton Oval. What stuck in my mind was a newcomer with a flowing action who at the end of the day, after opening the bowling, had none for a hundred. Then, with a final flourish, he yorked a tailender. I can still see him completing his follow-through as the ball crashed against the stumps. Lindwall was the name.

Afterwards I had to write a letter, ostensibly from my father, explaining that gastric trouble had kept me from school. I had no more qualms writing it than when I rose from bed, while home with flu or some such ailment, to practice bowling in the backyard once my mother left to do the shopping. My passion for cricket made it a peccadillo which would receive ample absolution from Curtin.

Wallace sat on one of the front desks. "Liam," he asked offhandedly after reading my letter, "how do you spell 'sincerely'?"

"S-i-n-c-e-r-l-y" I answered promptly.

"Good," he said, "you've always fancied yourself as another Keats. And how does your father spell it?"

"S-i-n-c-e-r-l-y, sir." Bravely, but my voice was disembodied. "We all spell it that way in our family."

My classmates had not enjoyed themselves so much since Wallace, by his hectoring, last reduced the refugee boy in our class to a confused stammerer.

"I want to ask your father about that Liam," Wallace said, pronouncing my name "Lie-am" and giving me one of his meaningful, above-spectacle-rim looks as when he told a transgressor to stand under the classroom clock, adding, "When the clock strikes, son, I'll remember you."

Curtin had forestalled that meeting and extracted a promise from Wallace that the episode would be forgotten.

But there was no saint who could stop Wallace meeting my father on his return from Sydney, which was why I invoked instant divine justice that Friday. Although I was too close to foresee it, it is not hard to imagine what happened when my father did meet Wallace.

I had wanted the angel of the Lord to transfix Wallace in mid-accusation. I had wanted the trumpets sounding, as I had dreamt of them, over the Dandenongs for some seconds before it dawned on voluble Wallace that the time for bluff was over.

But Christ was not on call. I should have had more faith in my father who art on earth. Mild-mannered, respectful, he bridled at a Corcoran being bawled out for sticking to his rights. I had briefed him well.

Predictably Wallace, his main attack repulsed, smeared me with what he had promised to forget, my forged note with "sincerly" misspelt.

I realized it only later. My father returned from school in a glow of Corcoran pride obvious as he told us about the confrontation. However he was slightly reserved with me, which I understood only when my younger brother Tim began to play a spelling game.

My father, deep in a murder mystery, asked Tim to spell "sincerely," which he managed.

"You're the only one of us who's not a famous ignoramus, Tim. You've saved the tottering Corcoran reputation. It's even more important," my father continued sweetly, "to be sincere than to know how to spell it."

Touché for both Wallace and myself. I was suffused by anger as well as regret. Had my father claimed to misspell "sincerely" to save my face? I was too ashamed to ask. And furious with Wallace for breaking his promise.

It was a beginning of wisdom. My expectations had been perfervid, but Christ was not around the corner. Instead we have to make do with the Wallaces, the Curtins. I had to recognize that we depart while the world remains. The end will not come with a trumpet blast. Time does its insidious work imperceptibly. It hit me hard the other day when I saw the veins knotted in the back of my wife's hand. It's the heat which does it: I'm sure it's so oppressive because of car fumes. I think of her, of us, as unchanging but those veins showed time is shadowing us, hardening the arteries, silting the heart whose beats—when you reflect on it—are quantifiable and running to their term.

That is why the Witnesses at the door reminded me of that radical hope: that sometime He would come; that Time, stealthy enemy, would not have the very last laugh; that its imperceptible erosion would have a stop. Even some Buddhists will know what I mean.

Desmond O'Grady is the Rome correspondent for the Melbourne Age *and the* Sydney Morning Herald. *His stories, published in Australia, the USA, England and the Philippines, reveal a skilled craftsman able to perform equally well with serious or humorous material, a talent to watch. Mr. O'Grady appeared in SSI No. 26 with "Life, Debts, and Miracles of F.X. Horgan."*

"Wang's wife, Wang's wife, don't put on that act for me."

A Sunless Morning

BY LI GUANGTIAN

IT was eight in the morning and there was a heavy mist.

Wang's wife, carrying the laundry, stepped uncertainly out of the yard. She raised her swarthy face to gaze at the sky where the sun should have appeared, unconsciously shading her eyes with her left hand. Then wrinkling her brows she thought: Still such foul weather!

Lowering her head she made for the well. A big rooster standing on the winch beside it had stretched its neck to crow. Still crowing, it flapped alertly to the ground, just in time to avoid the pestle she threw at it. Shaking its blood-red comb from side to side, it fled, half flying, half running, apparently still crowing.

"Drop dead! Crowing cheerfully, aren't you!"

While swearing, Wang's wife bent down to retrieve her pestle.

Worried and angry, she had a bellyful of resentment to work off. With the weather so bad, of course the clothes wouldn't dry. But that didn't matter; her mistress had an iron and charcoal, so that clothes needed in a hurry could be ironed dry. That dratted rooster had left droppings on the winch; but although this annoyed her, it was nothing out of the way. Today something else was preying on her mind. The sight of the cock crowing so lustily made her think indignantly: Damn you! I suppose you're so cock-a-hoop because the Huangs' hen was killed instead of you.

Besides, since she woke at dawn, she'd been unable to forget last night's dream.

She had dreamed that Gouer's dad, his face streaming with blood, was standing before her.

"Look, Old Master Mao has let me go after all. He says I wasn't the one who stole those green jade bracelets."

Tears started to her eyes and coursed down her cheeks. In weeping she found relief. Yet she felt sick at heart, knowing quite well that Gouer's dad was dead, so how could he come back? Had she only dreamed he was dead? Surely not. She felt thoroughly confused. Before she could question him she heard him say:

"I must first go to thank the master and mistress for letting me off."

He turned to go to the family's living quarters. She knew the master was smoking opium right now and shouldn't be disturbed, so she tried to stop him. But he shoved her so hard that she fell to the ground, and at that she woke up, tears still in her eyes. She lay in bed at a loss, listening to the breathing of Gouer fast asleep beside her, and watching the pale light filtering through the window. She couldn't go back to sleep.

Her heart was like tangled hemp, and the more she tried to sort things out the more confused they seemed. She wanted to have a good cry, but something stopped her. Wide-eyed, she just made wild guesses at what had happened.

She thought: The death of Gouer's dad really made no sense. By the time she got the news, it was all over. She saw nothing but a cheap coffin. She was told he'd offended the master, had wanted to fight him, and the master had ordered the servants to give him a beating. Then he had rushed off to hang himself in the backyard. She wasn't even allowed to watch by the coffin, which they made frantic haste to bury. Thinking back to that day, she really blamed herself. Gouer's dad had said he wouldn't go to the Mao's house that day because he was feeling poorly, his heart kept beating wildly; but she'd kept on at him, saying that the landlord was giving his tenants a feast and would be settling accounts. He might be raising the rent. It really wasn't right to stay away. Then he'd gone, and never come back. She was left on her own now in her misery. And at this point she realized she should never have come to work here. Still less should she have accepted those five hundred dollars from the Maos, because they weren't much help to her mother-in-law and Gouer. Though the Maos seemed to be making amends to the dead man's family, they were actually trying to cover up their crime. Just think, if you beat a man to death, how can you keep it a secret? So many nightmares she'd had! In each, Gouer's dad, his face streaming with blood, told her, "Those green jade bracelets of theirs *weren't* stolen by me. With all those tenants at the feast that day, why should he pick on me? They said I'd been in their rooms, but I hadn't!" But now there was no way out. To make a living she'd had to stay on here, though she knew this was really letting down her dead husband, especially when she saw those two greem jade bracelets on Mrs. Mao's plump white wrists. At the time she'd thought of taking the case to court, but people had dissuaded her. They told her, "Old Master Mao's in cahoots with the magistrate. They're forever drinking, playing mahjong and smoking opium together. So what chance would you have?" Now of course it was too late, everything was finished. The grass was already high on her husband's grave. At the thought of this, her eyes filled with tears again.

It was gradually growing light. Time to get up. But overcome by lethargy she couldn't even feel anything, let alone worry about Mrs. Mao cursing her for getting up late. Her mind was a blank. Not until Gouer suddenly turned over and went back to sleep did she come to her senses again. She wondered: Should I wake him and make him get up at once? I can't turn in early in the evening, and missing me he won't sleep; so of course in the morning he likes to lie in. After thinking it over she told herself: All right, let the poor kid stay snug at my side a bit longer; he may have to leave this afternoon. He seldom comes to town. So when he does, he doesn't want to go back. He's been here two days already. If I keep him on, Mrs. Mao will say something cutting. Remembering Li's wife, the kitchen-maid, had got the sack, she couldn't help thinking Mrs. Mao a Tartar. Unlike Old Master Mao, she got up early and turned in late to keep an eye on everything, on each needle and thread in the house, each grain of rice. Nothing escaped her eyes. She had all the household affairs at her fingertips. She could talk sweetly to the underlings, could play the gracious lady or act the tyrant. Wang's wife was really rather scared of her. And each time she thought of her, she seemed to see that pair of triangular eyes in Mrs. Mao's yellow face staring at her in the dark. The servants often said even the master was afraid of those triangular eyes of hers. Most likely. But she knew very well what a thin time of it Gouer had. He depended on his mum, hankered for food. Though he had his granny at home, a granny is never as good as a mother. And what did they eat? He was lucky if he could fill up on maize and sweet potatoes, not to say anything better. Here, though she had no time to cosset him, he felt safe if he could see her face, hear her voice; and how he loved eating Old Master Mao's white rice with her and the other servants. At home he was really too lonely, without even a chick, a pup or the like to play with, for they couldn't afford now to feed them. Most likely he just stared blankly at the paddy fields in front of their two-room shack; but the green shoots in those fields had been planted by another family. Soon after Gouer's dad had been killed, Old Master Mao had rented that plot to another tenant. Suppose she kept the boy here with her? She had thought of that, even of asking the Maos to find him some job; but the child was still too small. The master and mistress would never agree to keep him... These thoughts held her motionless as if benumbed. But it was no longer early, she had to get up very quietly for fear of disturbing the child sleeping so soundly. As she stood by the bed, the gray light showed his face distinctly. She thought: You're the spitting image of your dad. You've got his nose and mouth. That upset her again.

Her dream was still preying on her mind. So she vented her anger on the big cock-a-hoop rooster, remembering how the Huangs' hen had been killed in his place.

Old Master Mao wanted a chicken dish.

The cook told him he had only one old rooster.

The master said he wanted a tender hen.

The cook told him the Huangs had one, but weren't likely to want to sell it.

The mistress hearing this said sharply, "Never mind whether they want to or not. Catch it and kill it for me."

So the Huangs' hen had been killed.

Yesterday she had seen the cook chasing that hen, then blood spurting from its cut throat. Blood! That reminded her of her dream.

The Huangs had rented rooms in Old Master Mao's garden.

It was a very fine garden. Its house with two wings was elegantly furnished and had a large square courtyard shaded by trees, as well as flower beds, tubs of goldfish, stone tables and stools—nothing lacking. The Maos had previously held feasts there, but then the place had been abandoned. The fish pond had dried up, the flowers had withered, the ground was littered with fallen leaves and dead grass. Mr. Huang was a teacher from another province, hardly ever at home in the daytime. His wife looked after the house and their little girl. As there were many trees and insects in the garden, she kept a small hen, hoping it would eat the insects and lay eggs. It would be a pet too for the child. At first they had felt quite secure here. But then Mrs. Huang learned a secret, after which she kept blaming her husband. It was Wang's wife, the washerwoman, who had let the cat out of the bag. One day in secret she asked:

"You know about that plum tree, Mrs. Huang?"

"That plum tree? What about it?" She sounded surprised.

"The Mao's second daughter hanged herself on that tree. Don't tell me you didn't know?"

Mrs. Huang hadn't known. Her husband had kept it a secret, because he wanted a house with a low rent, and he liked this quiet courtyard. But now the secret was out, his wife lived in daily dread and often said she heard strange noises at night. As to the way Miss Mao had hanged herself, accounts differed; but the concensus of opinion was that it was over her marriage, because that young lady believed in the new fashion of "free marriage," while her father and mother wouldn't hear of this.

Wang's wife often went in her spare time to chat with Mrs. Huang, and on the sly sometimes used leftover material from the Mao family to make little shoes or a cap for her daughter. With the money she earned this way, added to her wages, she could buy food and other necessities for her mother-in-law and son in the country. She often gossiped to Mrs. Huang too about her master and mistress. Their family was the only place where she could let off steam.

She had just laid hands on the winch, meaning to draw water. The winch wobbled, then was still, because another thought had occurred to her. The mistress hadn't come out yet, and with the weather so bad she really was in no mood to start washing. Instead she wanted to go to find Mrs. Huang and tell her: Old Master Mao ate your hen; but if you know what's best for you, don't make a fuss about it, otherwise there'll be trouble. A landlord's entitled to eat his tenant's hen. She also wanted to tell her: Old Master Mao told his wife to warn you on no account to let your little girl pick any flowers in the garden, because if she broke off the branch of a tree a grown-up in his family would die; if she broke off a twig one of their children would die. Another thing she wanted to tell her was: One day Mrs. Mao told the servants: Living here, the Huangs should show a bit more tact. I don't mind them drinking water from our well, but they should provide their own rope. Other people mustn't use the Mao family rope. And she'd tell her: Last night I dreamed about Gouer's dad...

But just as she arrived at the garden gate and was reaching up to knock, she discovered that it was locked. That puzzled her. Why should the whole family have gone out so early? As she hesitated, she suddenly heard a shrill cry from the main hall:

"Cheap trash! Get out of here!"

Wang's wife recognized Mrs. Mao's voice, and wondered which of the servants she was angry with this time. Limply resting her right hand, raised to knock the door on its knocker, she pricked up her ears.

"Our home isn't an orphanage; we can't feed loafers, can't bring up trash. You've not only eaten our good rice and flour but stolen a whole vat of my preserved duck eggs!"

Wang's wife's heart missed a beat. "Can't feed loafers"—Could she mean...

And then she heard Mrs. Mao screech:

"Wang's wife! Wang's wife! Wang's wife!"

As if waking from a dream, she went through the side gate into the inner courtyard. The path under the veranda was flat and smooth, but she tottered as if on a rugged mountain track, each step costing her an effort. She heard a child crying. It was Gouer all right. His jacket thrown over his shoulders, he was wiping his eyes still blurred from sleep and sobbing. He made as if to throw himself into her arms, but didn't dare, because Mrs. Mao just behind him was in a towering rage. Her triangular eyes were dilated, her thin lips quivering.

"Wang's wife, Wang's wife, if you want to bring up your son, you can't stay here. If you want to stay here, send him home. What time is this to let your precious son lie abed? That's not the way in our house! You know how kind, how generous I am. I don't mind a child having a few meals here, but he should never, never have filched those forty eggs. Disgraceful! Just think, forty of them, all gone. He hasn't left so much as the shell of one!"

Gouer sobbed. Wang's wife hung her head, frowning. Her swarthy face turned deep purple. Standing in a corner well behind Mrs. Mao were four or five servants and maids whispering together, some with tongues sticking out in dismay, others scowling. A young maidservant at the back shook her finger viciously at Mrs. Mao, then slipped out. Mrs. Mao went on fulminating:

"The world's going to the dogs. Respectable families like ours have no way out. People come as they please to eat our food, drink our wine. How much food can I spare for outsiders? Everything costs the earth. Which family isn't hard up? And luck's against us. The authorities demand grain, the troops demand fodder. The new county magistrate has sent to demand fifty piculs of millet! Millet! I don't have that much!"

Wang's wife said nothing, biting her lips. Her silence infuriated Mrs. Mao.

"Well? Are you made of wood or stone? Are you deaf and blind? Are you dumb?"

Mrs. Mao turned to leave, but called back over her shoulder:

"Wang's wife, you've brought up a fine son, a real treasure. Forty of my eggs, and you don't say a word. I see you've no intention of laying a finger on that treasure of yours!"

While saying this she turned up her cuffs, and her green jade bracelets gleamed. Then she swept out of the hall like a gust of wind. The servants and maids who had been looking on hastily made themselves scarce.

Wang's wife felt ready to explode. Forty eggs! Let it be four hundred, four thousand, forty thousand. Unable to contain herself, she wanted to give vent to her feelings. But upon what? Gouer was standing beside her. She snatched hold of him and dragged him out below the veranda. As she grabbed a bamboo from the foot of the flower bed fence, the big red rooster clucked with fright and fled. In bewilderment Gouer cried, "Ma!" The bamboo landing thwack! thwack! on his bottom made a sound like firecrackers.

"A finger! A finger! See if I dare lay a finger on you!"

The bamboo rose and fell faster and faster, each stroke harder than the last. As she thrashed the child Wang's wife shouted, "I'll teach you to do that again!" The bamboo broke in two. As she threw it aside she heard that Gouer's intermittent cries had changed into continuous wailing.

She stood beside him, her hands on her hips, not saying a word, just panting.

The child's wails were growing fainter. Her heart softening, she thought, "Poor kid..." But then Mrs. Mao darted out again from the main hall.

"Wang's wife, Wang's wife, don't put on that act for me. I'm not afraid. If you kill him, I'll take the blame! Let me see you beat him properly!"

Before she had finished, Wang's wife had already tugged a big bamboo from the fence. Once more she pressed Gouer down, and thrashed his buttocks and thighs with all her might. He struggled feebly, wailing:

"Dear Ma, dear Ma, dear Ma..."

"Who's your dear Ma?" she shouted, beating him hard. "I bore you but I can't raise you. Today I'll beat you to death!"

By now Gouer was too exhausted to wail or to struggle. And she was too tired to go on beating him, but still she went on raising her aching arms, shouting intermittently, "I'll teach you to do it again!"

The big bamboo broke too, yet she went on beating him, because of the triangular eyes looking on malevolently from the side gate.

Footsteps were heard on the covered walk leading to the outer courtyard. The Huangs who lived in the garden had come back. Mr. Huang, in uniform, led the way followed by Mrs. Huang holding her little girl's hand. Behind were two porters they had hired to carry their luggage. Today was Sunday; they were going to move house. Mr. Huang had taken his wife to look at their new quarters. After Wang's wife had told Mrs. Huang the secret of the ghost who had hanged herself, and after Old Master Mao had eaten their hen yesterday, Mrs. Huang had complained so endlessly that Mr. Huang had to comply with her wishes and move out at once.

When Mrs. Huang saw Wang's wife beating her son so hard, she wanted to intervene, but seeing Mrs. Mao there she thought better of it. Paying no attention, she hurriedly led her daughter off to open the garden gate. Mr. Huang, to show his good manners, inclined his shaggy head towards Mrs. Mao, and forced a wry smile on his pale face as he said:

"Good morning, Mrs. Mao. Please tell Mr. Mao that we're moving out today."

Mrs. Mao, her triangular eyes slightly narrowed, answered:

"I see. Please drop in to see us later."

She spoke rather abruptly, feeling put out. Without waiting for Mr. Huang to say any more, she turned and went back inside.

Meanwhile Wang's wife had long since stopped raising her arm. She tossed the broken bamboo away and flopped down to sit by her son. Covering her face with both hands she burst out sobbing.

The mist was still very thick. The rooster gave a long crow by the well. By the time Old Master Mao, his back bent, shuffled out from his room in his bedroom slippers, the sun happened to show its face from behind the mist. It shone on Old Master Mao's livid white face, making him look like a corpse.

At lunchtime the servants and maids in the kitchen talked things over. They talked of Wang's wife, Gouer, the green jade bracelets, the forty eggs, the new county head, the official levy of millet, the Huang's hen, their moving house, the ghost of the girl who had hanged herself, the misty weather. "The sky's always overcast!"

they swore. By this time Wang's wife, a bundle on her back, Gouer's hand in hers, was walking firmly, lips pursed and scowling, across the far-stretching wasteland.

Soon after his birth in 1906, Wang Xijue's poor peasant family "lent" him to his middle-aged sonless uncle who changed his name to Li Guangtian. Li was not free from cold and hunger in his youth. His strong motivation for schooling took him to Beijing University from which he graduated. He taught, edited and wrote prolifically. His early writing is noted for its bucolic flavor; his later work sets forth his concern for the democratic movement in China. He was Chancellor of Yunnan University for 16 years and then tortured by the "gang of four." The story was translated by Gladys Yang.

"My private affairs are sitting in the back seat."

The Chief Clerk

BY E.G. PEACOCK

MR. Sinnamuthu sat impassively at the ink-stained teak desk, his ample belly resting comfortably against its edge. Circular gold-rimmed spectacles perched on the bridge of his squat nose. Through the half-open door of the inner office he could just see Tuan Pitman, the Penang manager of Livingstone & Spencer Limited, spreading files across his desk while Chattaway, the new relief manager, bent over them and occasionally asked a question in a low voice. Outside, the din of the waterfront provided a contrast to the cloister-like hush of the office.

Mr. Sinnamuthu sighed and inserted the end of his pen into his right ear and rotated it slowly. This habitual action together with his expression of deep thought gave the impression that he was winding up some clockwork mechanism within his round and almost hairless head. The soft whirring which came from the overhead fan completed the illusion.

He was still pondering the problem of his imperative need to visit Kuala Lampur in the future when he was interrupted by the sound of the swing doors that led to the outer corridor. Rashid, the office *peon*, backed through them into the room bearing a tray on which stood two cups of *kopi-oh* from the coffee stall under the Japanese cherry tree just outside the office.

"Mari sini," commanded Mr. Sinnamuthu.

Rashid stood by Mr. Sinnamuthu's desk while the latter, as was his custom, tested the temperature and sweetness of the brew by the simple method of dipping a plump forefinger into each cup in turn and then into his mouth, rolling his eyes heavenward as he did so.

"O.K.," said Mr. Sinnamuthu, and Rashid carried the tray into Tuan Pitman's office and laid it on the desk with a flourish that slopped more of the gray liquid into the saucers. Then he went out, closing the door after him. Mr. Sinnamuthu flashed him a dark look of annoyance at this frustration of any further chance to eavesdrop on the revelations which Tuan Pitman must be making to Chattaway. Rashid ignored him and left the office to resume his interrupted game of *sepak raga* on the open space by the godown.

"Damned fool," Mr. Sinnamuthu murmured to himself in English as he picked up the letter he had been painstakingly composing for most of the morning. Moving his lips soundlessly, he read over what he had written, pausing from time to time to make a correction in his careful copybook script. When he was satisfied he began to make a fair copy.

C.L. Pitman, Esquire,
Manager,
Livingstone & Spencer Limited.

Sir,
I have during the weekend been the victim of a nasty accident in which I nearly lost my life owing to the recklessness of a Georgetown municipal bus driver who allowed me to pass by a signal and then suddenly swerved to the right, knocking my left mudguard at the tail. This threw the car into a violent skid on a rainy patch of tarmac which was not visible. The car went into space

twenty feet and landed flat on its four wheels on the top of a bush. During this brief fraction of a second I braced myself by depressing with all my might the clutch and brake pedals and my hands were perpendicular to the steering and my back torso was pressed tightly against the seat. I reckoned that in this manner my ribs would be saved. The experiment worked and I came out calmly by opening the door. If I had not pressed the clutch the wheels would have kept spinning and the car would have run amok in the orchard.

With the assistance from three bystanders I started my car and with a little difficulty due to mud managed to weave my way through the ditches and the trees and reached home where I began to develop the usual shock symptoms. Since that day my consumption of cigarettes has increased to a tin a day due to nervous reaction.

Being a photographer of some standing I need time to take photographs of the scene of the accident, the car, photomicrographs of the twisted metal for a report from the metallurgist on the fitness of the car for use on the road in view of the twisted steel which has sustained metal fatigue. On these microphotographs will rest my case for a new shell for the beetle from Wolfsburg.

I need fifteen days leave to take the car down to Kuala Kumpur to see the German auto engineer in Supreme Motors Limited to examine my car thoroughly for the alignment of the shell on the steel-plate chassis. In view of the fact that when the impact occurred smoke emanated from the steel body and IMMEDIATELY thereafter the car plunged into a bush full of cold rain water. This, any technician will explain with common knowledge, is a classic example of steel losing its temper and becoming useless for protection against any future collision even at ten miles an hour.

I realize that, after having returned from annual leave ten days ago, I am putting you in a rather embarrassing position. However the situation just related is in the lap of the Gods.

Your obedient servant,
D. Sinnamuthu,
Chief Clerk.

Mr. Sinnamuthu put down his pen and looked at the clock on the wall. As he did so the door of the inner office opened and Tuan Pitman emerged, followed by Mr. Chattaway. Mr. Sinnamuthu prised himself away from the desk and rose to his feet.

"Ah, Mr. Sinnamuthu," Tuan Pitman said jovially, "you have already met Mr. Chattaway. I leave him in your capable hands. For the month that I am away I expect you to look after him and show him the ropes. I know I can depend on you." There was an almost imperceptible trace of bravado in the tone of this last sentence, as though Pitman knew he was tempting fate.

Mr. Sinnamuthu modestly cast his eyes downwards. "It would be my pleasure and duty to do as you ask," he said. "Regretfully a matter of some importance has arisen." He proffered the letter and Tuan Pitman took it reluctantly.

There was silence while he read it, except for the creaking of the fan and the muted sounds from outside. The paper in Pitman's hand shook slightly. Then he put the letter down and gazed into space.

"It won't do," Pitman said shakily. "It simply won't do. You have just come back from leave. Besides, I need you to assist Mr. Chattaway here."

The three men looked at each other, and for a few moments nothing was said. At last Tuan Pitman broke the silence.

"Where is it then? I want to have a look at it."

"At what?" Mr. Sinnamuthu inquired innocently.

"Your car, of course." Tuan Pitman turned an appealing look on Chattaway.

"It is outside," Mr. Sinnamuthi said guilelessly. "Where I always keep it." He waved a podgy hand vaguely.

"Then let us go and inspect this wreck." There was an edge of irritation to Pitman's voice and he turned brusquely, leading the way through the swing doors, along the corridor to the front entrance and out into the bright glare. Chattaway and Mr. Sinnamuthu followed him obediently.

The three men gathered round the rather sad-looking Volkswagen which was parked just outside the front entrance. Its black paint was dull and hatched with scratches; here and there it was blistered and rust showed through. There was an assortment of dents on all four wings and the front bumper drooped disconsolately.

"It doesn't seem to look any worse than usual," Tuan Pitman observed with an attempt at sarcasm. "Where is this twisted metal you wish to photograph?"

Mr. Sinnamuthu spread his arms and furrowed his brow with some difficulty. "The really serious damage is not visible," he said, gravely. "As I explained in my letter it is the loss of temper of the steel shell occasioned by—"

"All right, all right," Tuan Pitman interrupted hastily, "I haven't got time for all that. I have a plane to catch. You will just have to sort this out with Mr. Chattaway. But I really do not see the need for any more leave, especially at a time like this. It is most inconvenient and with Mr. Chattaway being new, not only to the office but also the country..." He raised his narrow shoulders in a gesture of finality.

Mr. Sinnamuthu's solemn expression slowly gave way to a reassuring smile. "Do not worry, sir," he said. "I know my duty. My private affairs are sitting in the back seat. Mr. Chattaway shall not lack a guiding light." He reached up and placed a protective hand on Chattaway's shoulder. "Go to your aeroplane with a clear conscience."

For want of a better response Tuan Pitman snorted and turned in the direction of his waiting car, his shoulders more slumped than usual. Chattaway and Mr. Sinnamuthu watched the car draw out into the waterfront traffic, narrowly avoiding a *trisha* which appeared from nowhere. Then, as one, they turned and reentered the office.

The somnolent afternoon drew to its close. The sounds of the street died down and the humid heat of the day lay over Penang like a smothering blanket. The clacking sounds produced by Betty Chan, the overweight Chinese typist, had diminished from her pre-tiffin crescendo of twenty words a minute to an occasional tap like a surfeited woodpecker, interspersed with heavy sighs. Mr. Sinnamuthu pushed aside the petty cash account on which he had been working and extracted from his pocket a large yellow handkerchief with which he delicately dabbed his forehead. Because yellow was the royal color of the Sultanates, Mr. Sinnamuthu felt that the handkerchief somehow reflected his importance as Chief Clerk of Livingstone & Spencer. He rose ponderously from his chair and waddled over to Betty Chan's desk. She took her fingers from the keys of the typewriter and regarded him sourly. It was part of the daily ceremony.

"You have finished?"—it was halfway between a question and a statement.

Betty Chan did not reply. She left the unfinished letter in the typewriter, dropped the P.V.C. cover over it and crammed various possessions into her handbag. Smoothing her *samfoo* she left the room without a word to Mr. Sinnamuthu, who gazed impassively after her departing form before turning to knock on the door of the inner office.

When he entered, Chattaway was hunched over a desk strewn with files. "Oh, it's you, Mr. Sinnamuthu. Sit down, won't you. I shan't be a minute."

Mr. Sinnamuthu eased himself into the visitor's chair and took a packet of cigarettes from his shirt pocket. "Do you mind if I smoke, Mr. Chattaway?"

"Not at all," Chattaway said as he tidied the files.

"It is for my nerves," went on Mr. Sinnamuthu conversationally. "Since the accident, you know. I mentioned it in my letter."

Chattaway looked up. "Oh, yes. The accident. I have just read the letter. You were lucky indeed."

"Not lucky," observed Mr. Sinnamuthu, drawing heavily on his cigarette. "Perhaps a combination of providence and ancestral memory."

Chattaway raised his eyebrows. "Ancestral memory? I don't quite understand."

"Ancestral memory," Mr. Sinnamuthu explained patiently, "is implanted in the genes and passed on from generation to generation. As a student of the laws of nature, you understand, I am familiar with such things. A bird is not taught to build a nest, it knows from the experience of its ancestors. My father was a motor-driver of great expertise. He was a taxi operator in Colombo and I have inherited his skill. It has saved my skin on more than one occasion."

Chattaway opened his mouth to speak but thought better of it. Instead he began putting the files away in the cabinet.

"You are staying, I believe, at the E. & O.," continued Mr. Sinnamuthu. "Perhaps I may have the pleasure of driving you there."

Chattaway was shrugging into his linen jacket. "Do not trouble yourself, Mr. Sinnamuthu. I can always take a taxi."

"No trouble," Mr. Sinnamuthu said heartily. "It is on my way. I just hope," he added ominously, "that the car does not let us down."

By the time Mr. Sinnamuthu drew up outside the entrance to the E. & O. Hotel, he had amply demonstrated his skill, if not his expertise. Chattaway climbed thankfully out of the vehicle.

"Thank you for the ride," he said. "It was very kind."

Mr. Sinnamuthu inclined his head. "It was nothing. Tomorrow I shall pick you up here at eight."

"Oh, no," Chattaway protested. "There is no need. I shall—"

But Mr. Sinnamuthu waved away his objections. "But I insist. Tuan Pitman wishes me to look after you and I pass this way. Also I would like to offer you the hospitality of my poor house after office. My wife makes a very excellent Ceylon curry. You shall be my guest."

Before Chattaway could reply Mr. Sinnamuthu let in the clutch and the car jerked out into the traffic.

Mr. Sinnamuthu bathed carefully, sluicing the cool water from the earthenware *tong* over his body. Then he donned a pair of white cotton trousers and a loose shirt and went into the house for his evening meal. Mrs. Sinnamuthu placed the dishes before him on the table and stood looking at him.

"You will be leaving for Kuala Lumpur in the morning?" she asked.

"No," replied Mr. Sinnamuthu through a mouthful of curry. "I have had to postpone it. I am needed urgently at the office."

"But you must go," Mrs. Sinnamuthu said petulantly. "You know what will happen if you do not. Your brother will certainly see that you do not get your rightful share. He is not to be trusted in your absence, that one."

"Quiet, woman. Do you think I do not know that? Do you take me for a fool?"

Mrs. Sinnamuthu sniffed but she said no more and went to fetch coffee, leaving Mr. Sinnamuthu glowering and thoughtful over his meal. When she returned he told her about his invitation to Chattaway.

"Make a good curry," he said. "Like your mother used to make." Then he collected some tools and went to attend to the car. It was late when he was satisfied with his work and Mrs. Sinnamuthu was already in bed.

The next morning Mr. Sinnamuthu stopped at the E. & O. as arranged to pick up the apprehensive Chattaway. On the way to the office Mr. Sinnamuthu weaved in and out of the morning traffic with reckless abandon, hurling imprecations in various languages at tardy pedestrians and obstructive bullock carts; Chattaway clung tightly to his seat. The daily routine of the office was dull by comparison and the hot hours dragged by. At last the time came for Mr. Sinnamuthu to release Betty Chan from her labors and once more he knocked on the inner office door.

Chattaway put down his pen as Mr. Sinnamuthu entered and suppressed a groan. He was not looking forward to an evening of Mr. Sinnamuthu's hospitality and even less to his driving. "Is it time already?" he asked.

"Indeed it is, yes," Mr. Sinnamuthu answered expansively. "The toilsome day is past, and I am looking forward to a jolly evening. You are ready?"

Chattaway nodded unhappily and together they left the office. At the car Mr. Sinnamuthu bustled round to the passenger's side to open the door for Chattaway. It stuck and Mr. Sinnamuthu gave a wrench whereupon the door came away from the frame and clattered on to the dusty road.

For long moments Chattaway and Mr. Sinnamuthu stood in silence gazing down at the detached door. "Dear me," said Mr. Sinnamuthu at last, darting a quick look at the bemused Chattaway.

"It is as I feared. The steel shell is beginning to disintegrate." He stooped to lift the door and Chattaway bent to assist him.

"Throw it on to the back seat," Mr. Sinnamuthu panted. "Fortunately it is unlikely to rain."

Together they maneuvered the door through the gap and settled it on the rear seat. Then Chattaway lowered himself gingerly into the passenger seat while Mr. Sinnamuthu climbed behind the wheel. He seemed relatively unmoved by the incident but Chattaway edged himself as far into the center of the car as he could and held on tightly as they drew out into the road, nothing but thin air between him and Mr. Sinnamuthu's potential victims. But Mr. Sinnamuthu made no discernable allowance for Chattaway's fears and vulnerability and, with what can be described only as verve, drove through the town, past the E. & O. and into the country where his speed climbed dangerously as the traffic thinned.

Perspiration beaded Chattaway's forehead when at last Mr. Sinnamuthu wrenched the wheel without warning and pulled the car off the road on to a rough track that led between trees to a nondescript wooden bungalow roofed with rusting corrugated iron. Mr. Sinnamuthu drew up in a yard of bare earth, amid a flurry of squawking chickens, and announced unnecessarily, "We are here."

Chattaway climbed stiffly out of the doorless opening and followed Mr. Sinnamuthu up creaking wooden stairs to a narrow veranda and directly into the sitting room of the house.

"Kindly make yourself at home," said Mr. Sinnamuthu, indicating one of two uncomfortable-looking armchairs on either side of a low table. As Chattaway sat down Mr. Sinnamuthu went to a back door and shouted in Tamil. There was an answering scream from somewhere at the back of the house and Mr. Sinnamuthu came back and sat in the chair facing Chattaway.

"My wife will bring us a cool drink in two ticks," he said. "The meal will be ready shortly. In the meantime, how do you like my domicile?"

Chattaway smiled weakly. "Very nice," he said, gazing around the small room. A bewildering variety of pictures hung on the walls. Luridly colored prints depicting various Hindu gods, a portrait of Sir Winston Churchill in bulldog pose, a picture of the Crucifixion, and one of the Buddha meditating a peepul tree. Mr. Sinnamuthu was taking no chances.

"Very nice indeed," repeated Chattaway and Mr. Sinnamuthu nodded his head in agreement.

"Modest but tasteful," said Mr. Sinnamuthu. "And half an acre of rambutan trees. You shall take some fruit back to the hotel when you go."

A very thin Tamil woman in a harsh pink sari and bare feet entered the room at the moment bearing a tray on which were two glass jugs, one containing a liquid of a poisonous green and the other a dark-brown concoction. Ice cubes tinkled in the jugs which were frosted with condensation. There were also two thick glass tumblers.

"Mariammah, my wife," said Mr. Sinnamuthu casually, as though pointing out a feature of but moderate interest. "She is uneducated and speaks no English."

Chattaway nodded uncertainly at the woman who glared back at him unsmiling as she unloaded the contents of the tray on to the table. The jug of brown liquid and one of the glasses she placed before Chattaway, the others before Mr. Sinnamuthu.

Chattaway looked questioningly at Mr. Sinnamuthu who reached forward and served him with the brown liquid; he then filled his own glass with the green. Lifting his glass, he regarded Chattaway expectantly. Chattaway took a cautious sip. A mixture of expressions flitted across his face.

"Fruit syrup," said Mr. Sinnamuthu, answering the unspoken question. "You will note that I am drinking a local lemon syrup but for you I have provided a European variety thinking that perhaps you would not find ours to your taste. It is our custom that nothing is too good for the honored guest," he added complacently.

Chattaway was thirsty and drank half the tumbler, which Mr. Sinnamuthu promptly refilled. "It is very good," he said doubtfully. "But I can't quite recognize it."

"Special European syrup," said Mr. Sinnamuthu. "Much more expensive than the local product. I bought it this morning just for you. California syrup of figs. He refilled Chattaway's glass again. "You have the whole bottle there, diluted with ice water." Chattaway went slightly pale but managed to smile his appreciation.

There was a pause in the conversation while Mr. Sinnamuthu noisily consumed his lemon drink. Chattaway pushed his glass to one side and sought for some topic with which to break the silence.

"Pity about the car," he said eventually.

"Yes," agreed Mr. Sinnamuthu. "But only to be expected." He shrugged. "I don't think that Tuan Pitman believed my diagnosis but it cannot be helped. If the car falls into pieces before I can manage to get it fixed, he will understand then. But it may be too late for me."

"But steel doesn't weaken as easily as that," Chattaway protested.

Mr. Sinnamuthu fixed him with a beady eye. "You saw for yourself how the door fell off. It is just the beginning."

Chattaway fell silent. There was nothing to be said. Before he could change the subject Mariammah was back in the room placing dishes on the dining room table at the other end of the room. A powerful odor of spices filled the air.

"The meal is ready," Mr. Sinnamuthu announced. He rose. "Come, let us eat." He transferred Chattaway's jug and glass to the dining table and brought his own. Chattaway eyed the food with further apprehension.

Mr. Sinnamuthu ladled steaming rice on to two plates followed by generous helpings of curried meat of indeterminate origin immersed in an oily juice of a fiery red. He pushed several saucers of dark chutney and unidentifiable oddments towards Chattaway.

"Please take some of this and that," said Mr. Sinnamuthu. "All are homemade from the finest ingredients."

Chattaway obediently did as he was told and raised the first spoonful to his lips, depositing the contents carefully in his mouth. Almost immediately an expression of total astonishment came over his face. Swiftly his jaws worked to masticate the mouthful and transfer it to where it could, presumably, do less harm. Beads of perspiration appeared like magic on his brow and his face turned a dark red.

Mr. Sinnamuthu himself ate with relish and appeared not to notice Chattaway's discomfiture. "Ah, yes," he murmured between mouthfuls. "Mariammah has done you proudly. This is one of her special curries. I can tell."

Chattaway fished for his handkerchief and mopped his streaming brow. His tongue and palate burned with an exquisite agony. There was only one thing for it. He seized his jug and filled the glass with the iced, brown liquid. Throwing discretion to the winds he swallowed the soothing draught, then another. Manfully he took another spoonful of the searing concoction. He did not want to give offense. Spoonful by spoonful, interspersed with gulps of syrup of figs, Chattaway reduced the mound on his plate and lowered the level of his jug. The veins in his neck knotted and those in his temples throbbed. Already his bowels were twisting in anticipatory horror at the corrosive substances being fed into his digestive system. He loosened his collar and tie and could only gasp and grunt at the table talk of Mr. Sinnamuthu. After an agony of time the contents of his plate disappeared and the jug emptied. Gratefully he placed his spoon and fork side by side and lay back steaming in his chair. He felt sure that his mouth and insides were as raw as a skinned rabbit.

Mr. Sinnamuthu gazed at him benignly. "Oh, my goodness, you enjoyed that, I can see. Let me help you to some more." He was already spooning out more rice and curry.

Chattaway made strangled noises and tried to wrest his plate from Mr. Sinnamuthu's grasp. But Mr. Sinnamuthu proved the stronger and the dictates of hospitality stronger still. The plate, replenished, was back in front of Chattaway. Once more he felt obliged to make the effort. Mr. Sinnamuthu looked on approvingly.

The second helping was scarcely diminished this time when Chattaway could take no more. "I am sorry..." he spluttered. The words emerged distorted by his inflamed throat. "Delicious—but cannot eat more." Wildly he patted his distended and tender stomach to indicate enjoyment and repletion. "Must compliment your wife. Never had such a curry." Breathless he stopped speaking, but kept his mouth slightly but indelicately open to allow the cooling air to soothe the ravaged tissues.

"I shall tell her," said Mr. Sinnamuthu. "But since you like our food so much I have a treat in store. The day after tomorrow I shall take you to see my cousin Veerappan. He is wishing to meet you and I promised you would come. His wife is an excellent cook, better even that Mariammah. And I shall procure more syrup of figs to take with us."

Chattaway waved his hand weakly and closed his eyes. The burning of his mouth and the churning of his stomach drove all thought from his mind except the appalling implications of Mr. Sinnamthu's invitation. They were too terrible to contemplate. As the rawness of his throat ever so slowly began to ease and Mr. Sinnamuthu's chatter swept over his head, a solution came to him. Pitman would be most annoyed when he returned but there was nothing for it.

"Mr. Sinnamuthu," he said, when an opportunity occurred. "I have been thinking. About your car. I am sure you are right about it being in a dangerous condition as a result of the accident." Chattaway's intestines gave a specially vicious contraction and he winced. "I am prepared to let you have extra leave to take it to K.L. for examination."

Mr. Sinnamuthu beamed. "But that is most kind. However, I would not dream of it. Tuan Pitman has placed his trust in me and I must stay and show you ropes. Also there is engagement for day after tomorrow."

"No," said Chattaway desperately. "No. You must go. As soon as possible. I wouldn't forgive myself if anything happened. It is all right. I can manage."

Mr. Sinnamuthu looked doubtful. "The car is undoubtedly a lethal instrument in its present condition. My cousin Veerappan would, I suppose, wait until my return. You are sure you can manage?"

"Yes. Yes, of course. You must go. I insist. I shall tell Mr. Pitman I insisted. Lose no time." Chattaway was babbling in his anxiety. A feeling of growing unease in his abdomen was convincing him that he too must lose no time, in reaching the sanctuary of the E. & O. "Now that is settled would you be most kind and return me to the hotel? I have an urgent appointment." Privately, he was not sure if he would make it.

 *A member of the Order of the British Empire, E.G. Peacock was born in 1926 in Scotland and educated in England, Hong Kong and Malaya. After World War II he joined the Colonial Service and worked in Malaya and Nyasaland (now Malawi). He was on the staff of American University in Cairo in 1977 and 1978. His story "The Way of His Fathers" appeared in SSI No. 29.*

"It was only when he was getting his
second wind that those nasty little doubts
had begun to nibble in earnest."

Case History

BY E.G. CHIPULINA

INCURABLE romanticism today may seem as anachronistic as the plague, but somehow Julian Gray had never responded to shock therapy. Even now, in his early forties, falling in love remained as inescapable and recurring a part of his life as income tax. And, incidentally, if he was still a bachelor it certainly wasn't a question of money. Perhaps it was his condition itself that worked against matrimony, for if he was chronically in love with Women-in-the-abstract, when the ideal suddenly materialized in a highly tangible form that slipped into his bed with scarcely a by-your-leave, well...something always seemed to go wrong. Oh, no question of malfunction; he relished the first exploratory tussles as much as the next man. But no sooner had he got his breath back than an irritating little doubt would begin to nibble at his ecstasy: was she really the right one after all? Even when doubt became certainty he was too gallant to come clean, so the thing tended to drag on unnecessarily.

Usually by the time his next tax return was due the tangible form had picked up the message anyway and shoved off of her own accord to a more likely bed. Then the cycle would start all over again.

Currently Julian was managing the Midlands branch of Grant, Bergson and Collins, Chartered Accountants, but it had all begun when as a very junior member of the firm he had been summoned by K.B. Grant himself and told: "Well, Gray, here's a chance to practice your Spanish. How would you like to do a spell in the Madrid branch?" which though formally phrased as a question was nothing of the sort. But Julian was delighted with the assignment. He had never been abroad before, and the travel posters of the day insisted that Spain was different. A couple of weeks later, as his plane touched down at Barajas, he was well on the way to discover that it was no idle boast.

At first he put up at a *pension familiar* someone at the office had recommended, a handy address just off Gran Via, a glorified flat with a homely smell of wax polish. It was run by a quiet man called Pepe, despite his wife. Apart from a coiffure like a wedding cake she was mostly midriff, used her lungs mainly as a processing plant for verbiage, and packed more into a single breath than Raymond Glendenning: how nice to have a young English gent staying did he have enough blankets breakfast would be served in his room he could come in late the street nightwatchman had a key but they were a *very* respectable house and of course he must ahem ahem refrain from inviting young ladies to his room...In the intervening sharp intakes of breath, Pepe conducted the business of the day.

Then it happened. On his very first morning in Madrid, Julian fell in love with the gorgeous creature in black and frilly-white that brought in his breakfast with a charming, "Buenos dias, señor," and left with a sidelong smile and a toss of her nearside hip. When on the third morning he asked the creature her name, she laughed.

"Carmela, of course."

It seemed to him the answer Juliet might have given Romeo. Could he take her out on her day off, to dinner...no? A cinema perhaps? Well...anywhere, then.

A pained expression had clouded Carmela's features. "Oh, impossible, señor. Forbidden. Don Pepe is *very* strict. I could lose my job." Whereupon she clinched it by walking off with an emphatic negative of her classical pear-shaped bum.

This was ridiculous! Why shouldn't the girl go out with whomever she pleased on her day off? He immediately suspected the hand of that garrulous baggage and her "refrain from inviting young ladies" etc., etc. Events, however, proved him wrong. Later, reassured by a sepulchral silence about the house that the baggage wasn't around, he went to have a quiet word about it with Pepe, only to stumble on a little love scene in the dining room. Carmela stood absently polishing cutlery, almost as if unaware of the salivary little nothings Pepe was whispering into her ear from behind, or of those hairy hands like spiders playing hide and seek in and out of her frilly apronfront.

The effect on Julian was traumatic. He found himself an apartment and checked out during the baggage's siesta time. Naturally, after a while he began to feel lonely. Unfortunately the colleague with whom he shared an office, a Canadian called MacDermott, wasn't exactly a pillar of consolation. It was difficult enough getting him to open his mouth at all, let alone talk about women—or broads, as he called them. They'd been out boozing a couple of times, but for MacDermott boozing ment just that, and his collected mutterances during a whole session hardly added up to a decent sentence. In desperation, however, Julian asked him: where did all the nice girls go in Madrid? How did you get to meet them?

MacDermott's laconic replies often had a sort of Delphic ambiguity that made Julian suspect he knew much more than he was willing to let on—he'd been living in the city a couple of years. This time it took the form of a profound "You don't" which Julian reasoned could have at least three possible meanings: (a) There are no nice girls in Madrid, (b) There are plenty but it's not easy for foreigners to meet them, or (c) There are plenty but squirts like you don't have a hope in hell of getting anywhere near them. Julian plumped for (b). Maybe it was only a matter of time—and the right connections.

Things brightened up a bit for Julian when, together with MacDermott and a senior accountant, he was assigned to the audit of a local concern. It was his first outside job and when he sounded MacDermott about it got the thumbs-up sign and a mystifying,

"They got class." Now in Spain at that time the vogue for independent auditing was only just beginning to catch on. Conservative bosses still reacted to the prospect with a sort of commercial prudery: "You mean to say we're going to let these people actually see our books?" Most of the rank and file too considered it obscene to have licensed peeping Toms at large on the premises. So when Julian, on top of having to unravel the cobwebs of a system last reformed by the Code Napoleon, found his simplest query parried with oriental evasion, he wondered what exactly MacDermott had meant by "class."

It dawned on him when, with equally oriental hospitality (expense account) they were all taken out to dinner at a five-star restaurant, where he was introduced to a very pretty girl with whom he instantly fell in love. Afterwards, losing the others, he invited the girl to a night club where they danced until the early hours. Then there was kissing and hanky-panky in the taxi home. And when they finally arrived at her flat and she held the door open for him his blood pressure went haywire. Unfortunately, in politely controlling a wild urge to rush in tearing off his clothes, he hesitated.

"Don't worry," she laughed. "It's all been paid for."

Another hesitation while it sank in that she didn't mean the dinner and—misunderstanding upon misunderstanding—the girl suddenly went all hoity-toity. "Now, look here, I can't take money for nothing. It's a question of honor." Eventually, of course, Julian did the honorable thing, but he had scarcely removed his pants when that doubt had already begun to nibble.

For several days afterwards Julian sulked in abstinence until he remembered the classical antidote to his misery. For a couple of hours he kept it up, shuffling dismally from bar to bar. But it didn't seem to work, and finally he rebelled. Life without women simply wasn't worth living; so if the nice girls were not available, well then, the others would have to do. He hailed the first taxi that passed, and hopped in.

"Girls," he demanded without shame. "Women!"

The driver, whether implying the ubiquity of womanhood or merely clearing the air inside his 1928 Citroen, made a sweeping gesture of the hand. Then, after a quick appraisal of Julian's suit, nodded, muttered something about mirrors, and set off at breakneck speed through unfamiliar sidestreets.

The mention of mirrors made sense when Julian finally found himself in a brightly-lit salon. For a moment he thought he had underestimated the virulence of Spanish brandy; then he realized he had stumbled on some kind of mini-Versailles. Tamely, he let a magnum-sized vintage whore lead him to the edge of a fake Louis XV armchair. And presently, at a delicate clap of her hands, a weird kaleidoscopic spectacle began to unfold before his eyes. It was as if a cattle show and a fashion parade had somehow got their fixtures mixed up and their respective organizers had agreed to compromise. The mirrors guaranteed that Julian missed no detail of the complex anatomies of the cow-models that posed for him in clinging garments that rippled with endless variations of the double-chin motif. Long before the show was over Julian had succumbed to the combined effects of brandy, heady perfume, and the illusion of being surrounded by menacing boobs. He staggered out, parrying the Mistress of Ceremonies's reproaches with vague promises of, "Later...later." But "later" found him in the nearest bar, finishing what he had originally set out to do.

At the office the following morning, racked by a terrific hangover, his spirits touched rock bottom. Still, as the old Spanish proverb reassures: God squeezes but does not strangle—or words to that effect. When he left that afternoon, as he passed by the open door of the insurance office on the floor below, he glimpsed a face behind a typewriter, eyes downcast as she powdered her haughty Castilian nose. He had never seen her before and he stood there on the landing, transfixed, until someone leaving shut the door.

All night long the face haunted him. In the morning he couldn't help blurting out his discovery to MacDermitt, who predictably said, "Huh," but was moved to eloquence when Julian declared his intention of getting to know her by hook or by crook. "Are you kidding?" Julian ignored him and determined to take up the challenge. Every afternoon at closing time he hung about in the street below, discreetly watching the exit of the building reflected on a shop window. As soon as he saw her leaving, he would stroll casually towards her and try to catch her eye. But she seemed to walk as if mesmerized by her toecaps. He couldn't even tell the color of her eyes. He took to following her and discovered that on most days a young man was waiting for her at the Metro just round the corner of the block. It was obvious from the way she mechanically hooked on to his arm and walked into the station with him that they'd known each other a long time. But Julian refused to be put off. Then he noticed that on certain days the boy friend didn't turn up— many Spaniards, he knew, had second jobs or put in overtime to make ends meet—and she would walk on towards a shopping area several blocks away, buy a few things or have a quick snack, then go into the nearest Metro.

Julian was growing impatient. This love-at-a-distance situation was beginning to pall—besides it was particularly frustrating to be so utterly ignored. Just a glance from her would have made some difference. At least he knew her name by then, having overheard a colleague call her Lola as he passed by the door of the insurance office. The next thing was to find out where she lived. So on the boy friend's next off-day, he followed her to the shopping area, then down to the trains and got into the same compartment with her. He got off with her and found himself in an old quarter of central Madrid where most of the houses had quaint little balconies or windows with wrought iron bars—a setting fit for Romeo.

As he went through this routine several times, the temptation to call on her grew irresistible. He racked his brains for a pretext, until Eros presented him with one in the shape of a small parcel that dropped from her handbag as she left the train. Julian pounced on it and followed her. He watched her enter the house, waited a few minutes, then taking a deep breath strode across the street and rang the doorbell.

A middle-aged woman opened the door. She could have been Lola's mother but he was too nervous to notice if there was any resemblance. "Er...is it possible to see the señorita Lola?"

He was aware of the curiosity in the woman's gaze, but he was used to that—it was his accent. Still, she answered quite civilly; "Come in. She has just arrived." She showed him into a cosy little parlor and offered him a seat. "She's probably freshening up a bit after the office but she shouldn't be too long."

"Of course." Julian said nothing about the parcel he was clutching, determined to hand it over only to Lola.

Left on his own, it occurred to Julian: if the woman was indeed the mother what was she thinking? Was she the my-daughter-right-or-wrong type or one likely to stir up trouble with the boy friend? The thought made him prick up his ears for any hint of male voices in the background. He was banking on the boy friend being late, but there could well be a father in the offing. Silence. God! What was she doing? It was like being in a dentist's waiting room—actually there was a small table in the middle full of magazines...Ah! That was the woman's voice.

"There's a young foreign gentlemen asking for you."

"A foreign gentleman?"

He sat up. That was Lola's voice. He'd never heard it before but it was just as he'd imagined it. The next moment, when he saw the girl who entered the room, he thought he had made a mistake. But it *was* Lola, only her hair was done up differently and she had changed into a sexy frock with a low neckline. And she was looking straight at him, smiling. He could see the color of her eyes now, hazel or greenish or something...

Details of the swift sequence of events that led him straight to her bed are not important. Of course, it cost him 300 pesetas like everybody else, but it was terrific. When he had regained the power of speech, he told her laughingly about the parcel and how he followed her every day. Was she aware that he worked in the office upstairs?

Really? No, she hadn't noticed him—no offense meant. She *never* looked at men in the street. Fiancés could get very touchy about that sort of thing. Besides she came from a *very* respectable family. Of course, what with the cost of living and the wages they paid...and anyway this place was so discreet! Afternoons only, silent visitors...

It was only when he was getting his second wind that those nasty little doubts had begun to nibble in earnest.

 *The multi-talented Gibraltarian E.G. Chipulina has a love for language and literature closely matched by his love for painting and sketching. He has been writing about 20 years, mostly short stories and historical articles which are published in prestigious magazines. His story "El Camarón" appeared in SSI No. 31.*

"She had taken him finally, on that great day,
into the magic cave of the underground."

The Yellow Line

BY S. KOMALA

EVERYDAY he went right up to the tip of that yellow line, never daring to put even a toe across. He would be immobilized, his eyes fixed on that line painted on the smooth hard concrete. The yellow line. That sacred yellow line.

He had learnt, parrot-like, the only English he had ever known from that yellow line.

"Please stand behind the yellow line, the train for Chater will soon arrive."

In the shiny caves of Hong Kong's modern new underground, the yellow line separated waiting passengers from the pits of the train tracks. The trains of the Mass Transit Railway moved people from the industrial outbacks of Kwun Tong in Kowloon, to Central, the business district on Hong Kong island. Chater station. Last stop.

He had never been to Chater. In fact, in all of his six years he had never been very far away from his home in Lok Fu low-cost government housing estate. What a day when the Mass Transit Railway opened! Everyone had rushed to try this new "Underground Iron"—the Cantonese name for the system. The people of Hong Kong had never seen a subway before. At least, not the people of Lok Fu Estate which was his whole world. How he had badgered his mother to take him too! Him too him too, he wanted to ride the underground iron! She had taken him finally, on that great day, into the magic cave of the underground. The mouth was near his home: the huge gaping mouth that swallowed him and his mother. And the funny machine spat out a golden ticket in exchange for a one dollar coin. He had stepped over the yellow line that day, and his mother had screamed at him.

"Stupid child! Do you want to die? Get back over the line unless you want to be killed by the wheels of the train!"

He had jumped back instantly. Never would he dream of disobeying his mother; he did not want to get beaten. The voice in the air spoke to him in Cantonese at that moment, warning him to stay behind the yellow line. Then came the English voice.

"Please stand behind the yellow line. The train for Chater will soon arrive." The droning, monotonous tones echoed around the station.

And then he saw the train! It came racing into the station, faster than anything he had ever seen. The big, shiny iron train.

How he had loved his first ride on the train! It had sped along so quickly. He knew that they were traveling far away. Maybe, even to another country. He had asked his mother whether they were going to China.

"Silly boy. You can't go to China on an underground train." But his mother had been smiling when she said this to him.

They had stopped at the next station, Kowloon Tong, but his mother would not go out of the station with him. She had insisted that they turn around immediately and take the next train back. His father would be coming home soon, and she had to prepare dinner.

"And you're not to tell your father I took you on the underground iron. He will get very angry if he knows that we have wasted money like this!" His mother issued the warning as they rode the train back to Lok Fu.

During all of the next week, he traveled on the underground iron. Everyday at three o'clock his mother would fall asleep, having drunk too much again. He would shake his mother, trying to wake her so that she would take him on the train. But she would only push him aside and tell him to go away. The first day, he had found his mother's purse and had taken two dollars, and had gone to the underground. His mother would not miss him, since she was always telling him to go out and play.

In the underground cave, he held his little golden ticket proudly. He knew how to get to Kowloon Tong! He was not actually sure where Kowloon Tong was, but at least he did know how to get there.

On that first day, he arrived at Kowloon Tong and stood at the exit: the foot of the stairs leading out of the underground cave. Against a blue, blue sky he saw a tree at the top of the steps. Did he dare? He was dying to know, to see this place Kowloon Tong. For a few moments, he hesitated.

And then he ran, for dear life, up those stairs. Outside he saw a wall surrounding a huge playing field. There were also houses, big beautiful houses; not like the tiny flat he and his family lived in. The houses had gardens around them and there were lots of trees. Most of all, he loved the big playing field. If only he could go into that field and run round and round it!

On the second day, he grew bolder and went up to the gate which led into the playing field. He saw some children playing there. They were foreign devil children with golden hair. How rich they must be because they had gold color hair. Everyone knew gold meant lots of money. Like his golden underground iron ticket which cost money. Money was important because his mother was always shouting at his father about money. Last night, he had hid under his covers as his mother threw an ashtray at his father for gambling again and losing money. These little boys had golden hair and didn't need any money. They were all happy and laughing. If only he knew how to get money!

The night of the second day he had watched his mother to see if she would notice that he had taken two dollars. She did not seem to miss anything. Good. He could keep riding his train.

"Please stand behind the yellow line..."

The third day, he watched excitedly as the train for Chater

arrived. Where *was* Chater? His friend in the next block had told him that Chater was on Hong Kong island. That meant that the train had to go through water. Impossible! He knew that trains could not run under water. He had tried to ask his father who ignored him as usual. On the third day the skies were gray and he thought it might rain. He walked further around Kowloon Tong, to see what this place looked like. If only he knew how close to home he was! He could not know though, for his world had always been just Lok Fu. There was one house he liked very much. It was big and new with a high wall around it. On top of the wall were pieces of colored glass. They looked very pretty. One day, he would live in a house like that too.

The next morning it rained very hard and his mother beat him with a stick because he had been singing too loudly. He knew he would be beaten that morning no matter what he did, because the night before his father had beaten his mother. Whenever that happened he could always expect a beating the next day.

The afternoon of that fourth day, he waited till his mother had fallen asleep and took his two dollars. Into the underground he ran, where he was sheltered from the rain. This time he did not go out of the station at Kowloon Tong. Instead, he played hide and seek with himself on all the different staircases of the station. He kept singing and singing; he was so happy because no one told him to stop. He walked along the yellow line and sang the English song about the yellow line. Just like the voice in the air that told passengers to stand behind the yellow line. He wished that it would stop raining so that he could go outside. But the skies remained dark and the rain continued to pour, washing his whole Kowloon Tong a dull gray.

When would his mother notice the missing money? She was always so worried about money, always complaining about money. In the streets in Lok Fu the next day he found a two dollar coin. Someone had dropped it near the bus stop. How wonderful! His ride on the underground iron on the fifth day would be paid for with his findings.

That afternoon, his mother heard him preparing to leave and looked at him sleepily. "Where do you think you're going?" she demanded.

He stood very still, afraid that she would stop him. He knew that she had not finished taking her nap and would fall asleep again soon. If only she would fall asleep quickly! He whispered that he was going out to play.

"Play, play, play! All you ever do is play. You useless, stupid boy. I don't know why you were born. You're too dumb to even go to school you ugly boy, just like your father..." Her voice trailed off to incomprehensible mumbling. Soon he heard a little snore, and he knew that she was sound asleep again.

Since he was later than usual on that fifth day, he did not stay in Kowloon Tong very long. He saw a boy with golden hair standing on a board with wheels and speeding along the pavement. He had never seen a skateboard before. What good fun it looked! He wished he could speak English to ask the boy to lend it to him for just a little while. He noticed that the train was very crowded on this day. Perhaps it was Sunday, the day many people did not go to work. To him, each day was much like the other.

He wondered why his mother seemed to be watching him very closely the next day. Perhaps she knew that he had been taking money. He did not know what to do. Riding on the train each day had been his greatest joy. That afternoon, while his mother was sleeping, he took enough money for two days. That sixth day he was scared, and stared for a long time at the yellow line as the trains passed him by. He put one foot over the yellow line, wondering if anything would happen. Suddenly, the voice in the air shouted at him.

"The little boy in the blue pants, please stand behind the yellow line!" He started and stepped back. He did not think anyone would be watching him.

That night he felt terribly afraid. Somehow he knew that his mother was going to scold him.

"You've been stealing my money, haven't you?" His mother shouted as she approached him menacingly. "Well, haven't you? I know you—you're just like your father. Taking my money and spending it. You're a bad boy!" Her voice was rising to a frenzy now. "I'll teach you not to steal again, I'll beat you!" She hit him hard, again and again and again. He cried out, "Mummy don't beat me. Please don't beat me anymore. I promise I won't steal."

She continued to beat him in a blind fury until the neighbors called the police and she had to stop. When her husband came home, he yelled at her for beating the child, and then he hit her.

He cried himself to sleep that night, knowing that he had only one more ride on the underground iron. His mother told him to stop whimpering.

On the morning of the seventh day, the sun was shining. He began to make a plan for himself. He would not be his mother's ugly boy anymore. He kept very quiet that day, so that his mother would ignore him. No singing, no laughing, no smiles. Nothing to arouse his mother's suspicions. When he knew his mother had fallen asleep, he took his last two dollars and ran to the mouth of the underground cave. Quickly, he had to go quickly very far away to his haven in Kowloon Tong. Only this time he wouldn't come back.

Kowloon Tong was so lovely on a sunny afternoon. Once again, he saw the boys with the golden hair and his favorite house with the colored pieces of glass cemented into the wall. He went as far as the bus station, where he climbed a tree. It truly was a lovely summer's day, and he was enjoying every minute of it. That last day he completely forgot the time. It would not matter if he never went back because his mother would never find him in faraway Kowloon Tong. All afternoon he played, rejoicing in the fact that his mother would now be awake and wondering where he was. He could sing to himself in Kowloon Tong. No one would stop him. Sometimes, people even smiled at him. He knew that they were probably thinking he was a clever little boy because he had traveled so far away from home all by himself on the underground iron train. He would live forever in Kowloon Tong station.

As it grew darker, he crept back into the brightly lit underground cave. Maybe he should go to Chater. He would have liked to visit Chater, to see if the train could really go through water like his friend said. But no, that would be too faraway. He did not know what the distance was, but he knew that there were many stations to Chater.

It was time to go home. He bought his golden one dollar ticket from the funny machine. Proudly, he walked to the train platform. He knew the way. No one had to show him because he was an experienced traveler on the underground iron. And on the concrete platform he could see it: the yellow line, that sacred yellow line.

He went right up to the top of the yellow line, just as he had done all week.

"Please stand behind the yellow line; the train to Chater will soon arrive."

The voice in the air sang to him first in Cantonese, then in English. Then he saw it: racing out of the tunnel was that fast, shiny underground train, speeding towards him.

In the distance, the motorman did not see the little six-year-old boy who stood so still at the tip of the yellow line among all the other passengers.

The train was coming closer now. He did not move; he hardly dared to breathe. As the train pulled swiftly into the station, he dashed over that yellow line, into the pits of the train tracks.

Sussy Komala, Indonesian, was born and bred in Hong Kong. She has been a "scribbler" since age 11. Several years ago she "forsook a life of luxury and comfort for the insecurity of my typewriter." She is presently in the USA but her heart belongs to Asia.

"Gyuszi was the 'lawyer' in our cell
for it was he who had been in and out of jail
at least four times."

Christmas in Hungary

BY PAUL-THOMAS M. SZABADSÁG

WE were three in Cell No. 12 on what is called Death Row. The place was the so-called Minor Prison within the huge Collecting Prison in Budapest where Cardinal Mindszenty was also imprisoned for years. The time was Christmas 1955.

Of the three of us only I was a political prisoner; both Laci and Gyuszi were common criminals. Murderers, that is. Evidently the prison was too overcrowded and, because of this, the warden put some of the political prisoners into the same cells where the murderers were kept on Death Row.

Laci, only 21, was the youngest in our cell. He had twice been sentenced to death and was waiting for the President's clemency. Laci was charged, together with his younger cousin, with having murdered an old woman who was a usurer. They had borrowed 50 Forints (about $2) from her and when they were returning the money, she demanded, besides the capital, an extra 50 Forints for her services. This excessive usury so infuriated the two that the old woman was killed.

Laci was a gypsy or at least one of his parents was. Of the three of us he was the gayest. More often than not there would be a smile on his lips, in his eyes—and, you would instinctively feel, in his soul.

Gyuszi was quite the opposite. I would say he was a born criminal, as he had committed nearly every crime forbidden by the Ten Commandments or punishable under the criminal codes. His latest had been the killing of a young policewoman. As he told it to us, he had a heated quarrel with a friend in a workmen's tavern; then came the poor policewoman trying to placate them. She tried to force them out at gunpoint, but Gyuszi jumped to take the weapon. In the ensuing struggle, the pistol went off.

His distorted moral attitude as well as his strange political outlook were best revealed by his reprimanding us for having made shoelaces of the ribbons we cut out of our foot-cloth—on grounds that we were damaging "state property." The irony and contrast were sharpened by the fact that four years before he had spent some time in jail—for stealing 70,000 Forints (about $2,800) of "state property." As for his paranoiac mind, he could tell the most unbelievable story with such personal conviction that you would believe every word of it. Only when these fantastic stories revealed a similar pattern and the same unvarying elements of violence, blood, murder and unspeakable horror—only then would you arrive at the conclusion that they were the creations of an abnormal mind. From that moment you really feared the man, because of his preference for the abnormal, for violence, and his total lack of moral restraints.

Gyuszi was the "lawyer" in our cell for it was he who had been in and out of jail at least four times. By now he knew all the procedures, the tricks of the trials, as well as the "techniques of hanging." (He liked to describe the latter at great length and very minutely, while Laci and I remained rather unwilling listeners.) Gyuszi knew, for example, that the "hanging days" were usually set for the 2nd and the 25th of each month.

We had safely passed the 2nd of December, though not without fear and anxiety. Strangely—or perhaps naturally—the future, the idea of continued life after the next hanging day escaped us completely. We tried to heighten, to prolong every moment of our precious present—though I am sure none of us did this consciously.

Laci would walk for hours up and down the cell (seven steps forward, seven backward) and would sing to us little known Hungarian folk songs or genuine gypsy airs. His voice was by no means extraordinarily good; in fact, it was slightly irritating because of his goiter. But what it lacked in quality it made up in warmth and feeling. For he sang from his heart, pouring out his soul, his emotions, his yearnings. While he sang, you did not even look into his eyes, for the sincerity and profundity of his emotions demanded respect, silence, and even a sort of admiration.

We especially liked one of his folk songs, a charming question-and-answer love-confession, originating in the region of NagyKálló and called "Kallai Kettós" (The Double Dance of Kálló). He would sing the first part, that of the male choir, rather seriously, even dramatically:

"Oh my darling where have you been?
For two days you haven't been seen!"

Then he would pause, eliciting suspense, while he slowly changed his expression to a pleasing smile. After that he would continue with the answer of the female choir:

"Into a pit I didn't fall,
In love with you, Oh, I did fall!"

The whole manner in which he sang reminded me of a once popular song, a favorite of my father's which begins:

"The soul of the musician is made of songs,
In it the heart of the whole world sings..."

Soon Gyuszi would rise from his bed and would in turn sing his favorite song. It was called "The Prison Ballad," and each verse ended with the refrain: "Oh my dear mother, oh my poor mother!" The subject of the song was a young man who left his widowed mother and his home rather suddenly. He fell in love with a bad woman, stole money to spend on her and finally landed in jail. There he was visited only by his mother. He received letters only from her. But, in the end, he truly repented his past and his sins. Then one day the letters and the visits stopped. He knew his beloved mother was dead. Therefore, when he was released, he went directly to his mother's grave. It was shallow, barren, and without decoration of any kind. So he stole again—but this time white carnations and roses for his mother's grave.

Here the ballad ended with a final, "Oh my dear mother, oh my poor mother!" Gyuszi, however, added to it yet another ending. The young man was caught stealing the flowers but instead of defending himself, he just sang the ballad and was acquitted.

After these song-flowers or song-harvests my turn would come. For some reason they had asked me to read aloud to them. They were very fond of Turgenev's Fathers and Sons. Before I started reading, Gyuszi would sit down on one of the beds, while Laci would pace his customary seven steps forward and backward. Except for this rhythmic monotony, they would in no way disturb my unfolding the story, page by page. I can say with all honesty that I have never observed such deep respect for a writer, have never witnessed such emotional response manifested for the written word. Maybe the fact that we had been engaged to Death moved us so profoundly when we escorted Bazarov's parents to the grave of their only begotten son, that what was so unreal to them was so meaningful to us.

There was a Hungarian writer whom we liked above all and whose book we were most reluctant to give out of the cell or to exchange for a worthless, though impressively thick book. For this reason we hid Bird-of-Daybreak (that was the inviting title of Áron Tamási's work) wherever we could. We had to do this because occasionally the guards would initiate a "hipis," that is a thorough search, and then exchange any books they found. Gyuszi had a great talent for hiding things; at various places in the cell he even kept a knife, wires, matches and nails.

The author of Bird-of-Daybreak was a native of that part of the old Austro-Hungarian monarchy which now belongs to Rumania—Transylvania. The writings of these Transylvanian authors are characterized by profoundly penetrating insight into the relations between nature and human beings and by truly sublime style. They breathe a deep sincerity and humility and possess a certain purity and charm, not unlike that of young virgins gathering flowers on a blooming mountain meadow.

We had long discussions on the merits of the main characters of *Bird-of-Daybreak*. Of course, these were not ordinary literary discussions. We just imagined ourselves in these mountainous surroundings, walking in the balsam-smelling pine forests, gaily chasing the sheep on the mountain tops or enjoying the unbounded freedom of the sheperds. For at that time imagination was our only escape and we wanted—oh! how desperately we wanted—to deny reality.

Soon after the afternoon readings, the early darkness of the winter would again descend on us—or, rather, on our souls. All of us became silent as if Death itself were reminding us that we were engaged to it. When the twilight slowly descended and the shadows lengthened, in these moments our thoughts always found their inescapable ways to the ultimate question which clouded our days. All of us believed in the hereafter and in these somber moments each of us rehearsed our defense before the Lord.

The other days in the Minor Prison did not differ considerably. Reveille took place very early, around 5:00 A.M. After breakfast we had our daily twenty minute walk in the prison courtyard. We always passed the spot where the empty concrete holes of the gallows were sunk into the earth, covered with rusty iron plates.

Immediately after the walk Laci would start his "conversations" with Éva who was one flight above us, among the female political prisoners. At the beginning I was the "signal man" to send and to receive the messages, for Laci and Gyuszi were rather poor at the alphabet and in counting. Later on Laci became quite proficient, even "fluent" in this prison-talk in which a certain number of knocks represented each letter.

I still remember how the first "conversation" started.

Laci: "Are you married?"

Éva: "No."

Laci: (Jubilantly clasping his hands, as if he had found a precious treasure) "Your sentence?"

Éva: "Eight. And yours?"

Laci: "Death."

Éva: "Do you hope?"

Laci: "Yes." (He waited a while, then went on). "My name is Laci. Yours?"

Éva: "Éva."

Laci: "I'm twenty-one. And you?"

Éva: "Nineteen."

Laci: "Are you pretty?"

The answer did not come immediately; in fact we thought that the guards had returned and she had to stop for fear of detection. But finally we heard her "message."

Éva: "I'd say I am."

Laci: "Your hair?"

Éva: "Brown."

Laci: "And your eyes?"

Éva: "Mischievous."

All of us received this with heartfelt laughter. Soon after that it became a daily feature, a blessed relief in our life, but to Laci it seemed to have meant more than that. For on the second day he insisted on my "flashing" the following message in his name: "I love you, Éva." In vain did I argue with him, urging decency or reminding him that he was married.

"Maybe she will be the last woman to whom I talk in my life. And I—I don't mean it seriously. But it's so good to say this to a pretty girl. And maybe she would remember me if I die."

Against this I could not argue. So I sent the message in the name of Laci: "I love you Éva."

Again no answer. We thought she was offended and Laci showed sincere remorse. But soon came the reply, one of the longest ones.

Éva: "Because of your sentence, you may do so while in prison. But be careful, my dear!"

It was so nice of her.

Soon after that Laci discovered that when Éva or one of her cell-mates sang in front of the window of their cell, she could be heard in our cell, only a flight below. Immediately went Laci's "message" followed by Éva's response:

Laci: "Do you like songs?"
Éva: "Oh yes."
Laci: "Your favorite?"
Éva: "Nights of May, Nights of Love."
Laci: "Want to hear it?"
Éva: " I certainly would."
Laci: "Then listen my darling."

Laci then went, no, he jumped, to the window, as near to it as possible, and sang the song, his first serenade to Éva. There was such impressive force in his song (though not in the volume of his voice; this had to be muted because of the guards) that it reminded me of the love-call of the woodcock, one of the most sublime manifestations of love in the animal kingdom.

And so the days passed, one after the other, and their fleeting tempo brought us nearer to yet another Hanging Day.

December 23rd passed rather unnoticed, though we were but two days from the fateful 25th. We had gone through another book and Gyuszi taught us a new song:

"My chestnut mare is grazing in the meadow;
How silently does the morning star glow!
Like the morning star is my true love glowing,
Like a quiet brook is my song flowing."

Soon I was again asked to tell a story. They insisted on these stories as children insist on their bedtime stories. First I told them film stories. Then, when I had run out of them, I related the plays I had seen and, when in turn, I had told all the plays I knew or saw, I revived the fairy tales of my childhood. But these, too, came to an end and later on I had to use my own imagination to invent film stories and tales full of romance, love, intrigues and fairies, but always in a peaceful settng. A happy ending was a necessity.

Then came the 24th of December, the day when Christmas is celebrated in Hungary and the eve we call "szenteste" (holy night). On that day all of us awoke suddenly and at the same time. Instinctively we had a foreboding of the oncoming tragedy. Like animals, we felt the approaching storm, well before its actual arrival. It was Gyuszi who reasoned that because the 25th of December would fall on Sunday, Hanging Day would be held one day earlier and would be transferred to Saturday the 24th. That is, Christmas Day.

Having decided this, we could no longer stay in our beds. We cleaned our cell meticulously, made our beds and waited for reveille. Though we felt it was well-nigh past 5:00 A.M., it did not come. Thus we knew that there would be a hanging today, Christmas Day.

Gyuszi, the expert in prison matters, immediately assured us that nobody from our cell would be hanged because, prior to the actual hanging, he would have been officially told about the rejection of the clemency petition and given a shave. But nothing more. No last request, no farewell letter allowed, no farewell visit by the wife or the mother, no last consolation from a priest. Just a shave. Just the appearance.

It was again Gyuszi who guessed that some political prisoners and the Old Uncle (this is what we called him) would be hanged from Cell No. 11, just to our left. He had been his cell-mate for two months and knew his case very well.

Old Uncle was a peasant (around fifty-five) and already a broken man. He used to walk right ahead of me during the daily walks, his two hands firmly clasped at his back while he was always gazing down, as if bowing to the inevitable. A small brown man he was, his face dominated by his huge moustache the two sides of which also bent downwards, giving a really tragic look not only to his face but to his whole person. Doom had certainly left its mark on this man, and we instinctively felt the full import and meaning of it. His occasional glances told us that he also did.

Whatever were their political crimes, we felt great pity for these doomed men, for it was just too cruel to hang them on Christmas Day!

But we knew it was useless to plead for mercy in this prison. As monstrous proof, Laci and Gyuszi mentioned to me this case: one day both of them had heard the hysterical crying of a young pregnant mother, a political prisoner, as she was escorted, or rather carried on her last journey to the gallows. "For God's sake let me give birth to my child and then I will gladly die! Let me..."

They hanged her. But her memory and her cries still haunted the inhabitants of the Minor Prison.

Our ears had never been so sensitive as on that Christmas Day. We heard, or rather felt, every opening of the cell-doors, every step of the guards. They were too many, but we knew that some of them meant the last opening for the doomed men. We heard steps and we could not utter a word, for these steps were too familar to us.

There walked these men to their own graves—to eternity.

Finally Laci broke the oppressing silence with a remark that moved me to the depths of my soul:

"You know those who will be hanged today will probably have the most beautiful Christmas."

"Why?" asked Gyuszi.

"Because they will see the little Jesus today," said Laci, with sincere conviction.

This character of Laci's soul, this naïve and purely emotional approach to the ultimate problems—and their answers—was a most rewarding revelation to me. It provided me with the conviction that simple men, the weak, the poor, and the meek have, by their very natures, their own sure guides to finding God and, indeed, life itself; and these guides lead them further to instinctive, unselfish care for each other's fate and suffering. I do not suppose they consider this *love* or even *charity* but I think that for these virtues they must gain the Kingdom of Heaven.

It is perhaps mainly because of this revelation, because of this conviction that I feel certain that if I had the choice I should still have preferred the company of such simple men as Laci during my stay in prison to that of political prisoners confining themselves to a strict intellectual approach and vainly philosophizing on the meanings of life and death.

It was by now 7:00 A.M. and still no reveille, no breakfast. Their delay was an unmistakable sign that something extraordinary was happening around us.

For a very long while deep silence fell on all of us. It was unnecessary to talk; all our thoughts were centered on the very same problem, the very same fate which had by now appeared among us in the Minor Prison in its full might.

It was Laci, again, who eased this oppressing atmosphere. "I think one of us will be moved to Cell No. 11 within a matter of hours. And my guess is that it will be you, Gyuszi."

And so it turned out. The door of our cell opened.

"Take your *cucc* (prison jargon for one's belongings) and come with me," the guard ordered Gyuszi. Incidently, this guard was called Hitler because he closely resembled his namesake.

Gyuszi took his soap, a little comb, his bread (that was all he could call his own). We wished him a hushed "Merry Christmas" and out he went.

I remained alone with Laci. In a matter of seconds we both heard the door opening to Cell No. 11 and very soon Gyuszi identified himself with his characteristic heavy knocking on the wall.

By now the time must have been around 8:30 A.M. Soon after that we got breakfast. Still we were not hungry, neither of us touched the bread but we drank the coffee, for it was warm and this warmth we needed very much.

Then came our daily walk. This time Gyuszi walked in front of us. But Old Uncle was not there. Nor some others. No more.

After the walk Laci and I ate our bread. Soon we were talking about Christmas and I happened to ask him, out of sheer curiosity, whether he knew the authentic story of Christmas, that is the story of the birth of Jesus Christ as told in the Gospels.

Laci did not even know what the word Gospel meant! Yet he seemed to be genuinely eager and interested to hear it from me. So I related to him those parts of the Gospels which described the events in Bethlehem.

We were still talking about the first Christmas Day when our dinner was pushed in through the small opening of the cell door, along with a cold supper, for the following day was Sunday. This supper consisted of a piece of bacon (always rancid) and a tiny bit of jam. As usual, we ate some bread with the soup. Following dinner Laci was kind enough to wash the bowls and after that he started his routine walk in the cell. I was reading a book and stopped rather reluctantly when he called for my attention.

"Paul, I'd like to tell you something," said Laci in a very serious voice.

"Well, sit down and let's hear it."

He apparently was in deep thought. And I, out of patience, repeated my "Let me hear it."

He waited for quite a while. Finally he said in a trembling voice: "You know, Paul, I didn't kill that old usurer."

"You don't mean it!" I seemed to have shouted.

"It's true, Paul," said Laci, now with a calm voice.

"For heaven's sake! Then who killed her?"

"My cousin."

"I don't understand. Why was he sentenced only to twenty years and you to death by hanging? Explain it to me!"

"Well, it's very simple," said Laci, by this time with a little smile playing on his lips. "I told my cousin to say that I was the murderer. And the court believed it."

I grabbed his shoulders and asked him: "But why?"

"You know, I have this heart ailment, made worse by a bad goiter, and the doctors have long ago told me that I have only one or two years to live. I thought I didn't have as much to lose as my cousin who is so young. That is why I did it."

"But—but you are now a father, you have responsiblities towards your family! You cannot deprive your son of his father. Think of that!" I argued vehemently.

"No, Paul, I've already made up my mind. I know what I'm doing."

"Did Gyuszi or anybody else know about it?" I asked him. "No, you're the first one I've confided in," was his reply.

"Laci, it's a very noble thing that you've offered your own life for your cousin but still you must not do that. Think again of your child. You should reveal everything, tell everything. It would be too cruel for you to die for another man's sin."

He waited for a while, as if my arguments had made an impression on him, as if he were weighing them, balancing them against his conscience—against his child.

But finally he stood up, giving added meaning and importance to his words. He said, as seriously as when he had confessed that he was not the murderer:

"No, Paul. Thanks for your care, but I'm convinced I'm right. And, besides, by now it would be unwise to reveal anything. For what could I attain by it? To have both of us hanged? No, let everything remain as it is."

I may have waited for a few minutes because he seemed to expect me to say more. But there was nothing more to say. Still wanting to show my appreciation to him, I just shook hands with him as one would do with a good friend, with an honest man. For he had become both to me.

I was so overwhelmed by Laci's revelations, by the new light in which his character now appeared to me, as well as by the dramatic events of the day, of this Christmas Day, that I just sat down, deep in thoughts and emotions. I felt that I had experienced mighty antipoles of life, like birth and death, boundless dimensions of the human soul as are only found in religious beliefs and personal convictions.

In the afternoon Laci resumed his "love affair" with Éva and soon he contacted her by wall-tapping, but without my assistance. This gave him much pleasure and joy. A little later I suggested that he send a Christmas greeting to Éva which he did immediately, very obligingly and enthusiastically. At this point I thought I might step into the "conversation" and I listened for Éva's return message.

"Thanks, and merry Christmas to you too! Don't give up hope. And sing some Christmas carols, will you? We're doing the same."

What a blessed idea it was. So with great joy and solemnity befitting the occasion, we sang each and every Hungarian Christmas carol we knew.

As if intending to bring us closer to the end of the day, darkness fell very early—or, perhaps in the excitement of our singing, we did not notice its sudden arrival. However it happened, it made me remember the Christmas customs of a free life. After the lights were turned on, I offered Laci my token Christmas gift, that is, if he wished, he could have my prison coat. (I saw him, two or three weeks ago, looking at it with great longing; he seemed to have taken a fancy to it, probably because of its newness and rather good cut. So I decided to surprise him with it on Christmas Day, though he had not asked for it.) Thus it came about that we exchanged coats and Laci, in turn, presented me with his own Christmas gift: his portion of jam. I hesitated to accept it, but he insisted and not wanting to hurt his feelings, I ate it immediately, except for a tiny bit of mouth-sweetener which I made him eat.

After that I retired to my beloved treasure: *The Poems of Robert Burns*. It seemed to have been an Act of Providence, that this Scottish titan was able to have his seeds, his flowers planted in the Minor Prison and have them come alive, as glowing and as vivid as was his love for that fairy creature, for Mary Campbell.

And what echo his eternal voice provoked this day! What harvest we gathered from his immortal seeds!

Once I mentioned to Laci how fond I was of Burns' poems and that I thought I would learn by heart my favorite, the "Highland Mary."

"Will you read it to me, please? I'd very much like to hear it," requested Laci with eagerness.

"No, you read it and thus you can help me memorize it," I suggested to him.

Then I gave him the book and while he was reading it, I tried to recite line by line, verse by verse the "Highland Mary," our first harvest of those immortal seeds. It took but little time to learn the poem.

We were so much embedded in the world of Scottish moors and lochs, so greatly filled with admiration for the love between Robert Burns and Mary Campbell, a love which was deeply woven into the birch-scented Highland background that we stopped only for a few seconds for supper (though usually supper was the main event of the day and demanded a certain ceremonial air).

Laci appeared to have been deeply moved by the last verse of the "Highland Mary" and often recalled the last two lines.

The day was crowded with events, tragic as well as momentous, the music of the immortal poet evoking sweet melodies in our soul, and, above all, the charm of Christmas Day was holding all of these with such a forceful embrace—as the night would embrace the dreaming trees of a pine forest or the winter's snow the silent meadows—that we just said a "Good night and dream of old Christmases"...and so passed a Christmas Day in the Minor Prison.

Epilogue: The following could not have been mentioned within the body of the story—for its time dimension is confined to thirty-eight days—but honor towards my cell-mates and respect and sympathy for the reader's curiosity demand that I tell that both Laci and Gyuszi received clemency and their death sentences were commuted to life imprisonment. This was subsequently confirmed by more than three fellow prisoners. During the Hungarian Revolution of October 1956, all the political prisoners, and I too, were freed by the revolutionaries. But not the common criminals. Both Laci and Gyuszi are still serving their sentences in a Hungarian prison.

Paul-Thomas M. Szabadság writes in English and Hungarian. For the last two decades he has done research and writing in two branches of the social sciences.

"Kwang had already turned his bull loose and stepped back."

The Sunny Side after the Harvest

BY KIM YONG IK

IN the tiny straw-thatched house, Yun Ho's mother lit her kerosene lamp against the early twilight of the harvest-time. Setting it on the table between the two rice bowls, she looked from the sullen face of her son to his untouched food.

"Why do you not eat?" she asked.

The red tinge of anger deepened on Yun Ho's neck, but he did not speak. Her voice was at once stern and gentle, like an early spring wind. "This new rice will not go into flesh and bone if you eat it in bitterness. Think now about the two sacks of rice more than we expected," she continued as Yun Ho still sat with tight folded arms and firm set mouth. "In your father's lifetime, it happened only once."

Yun Ho took a spoonful of rice and choked at once. "Bitterness!" he cried. "I will return this big bitterness."

She sighed, but only said, "How can you return bitterness to a man for refusing you his daughter?"

"I do not know." He made an attempt at eating but the rice stuck in his throat. "The matchmaking woman encouraged us all summer by saying 'The marriage talk is getting ripe for the ceremony at the new rice time.' Now the rice is in sacks, and what do we hear? The bull braggart has refused all summer to let me marry Doo Soo!"

Only today had the matchmaker revealed the opposition she had not been able to break down. Kwang's exact word she finally had reported. "This is the opening marriage in our family. The winner of the three village bull match cannot give his eldest daughter to the son of an obscure bean sprout woman. Rice and bean sprouts! His marriage money is not so much as one of my bulls."

The recollection was a new stab. He burst forth again. "I will show myself to this bull braggart! I will show him what I am!"

All summer he had poured pond water into the thirsty fields, stooped over to weed and shouted loud to scare away the hordes of hungry sparrows. He had gone to the mountains to collect enough firewood, so that he could give Doo Soo a warm winter at his house.

All summer Doo Soo had shyly avoided him. But she had smiled, showing all her dimples. Yun Ho had no doubt she liked him. Her quiet mother always talked to him friendly. But her arrogant father!

Yun Ho lifted his brass bowl and banged it down, scattering the rice. His jaws bit tightly on nothing. "I want a bull!" he shouted. "I will show him someone else can have a fine bull. One man is not better than another because he has bulls."

"You cannot behave like this before the steaming new rice," she cried unhappily. Then she counselled quickly, "Go over to the field Ahrn wants to sell and see if the land is good enough to hold water for rice. We will buy more land, and some day we can have a tiled roof, too. There are other girls besides Doo Soo."

He knew she meant for him to buy land with money they had saved for his marriage. It would have provided a fat porker and wine for the feast; a chest and silken clothes for the bride.

"I do not want land! I want a bull!"

His mother voiced her surprise. "Why in this world do you need a bull? You are not going to keep a bull in our house?"

"Yes, I want a bull, a strong fierce one that can win a bullfight even with the best of the bull-braggart's," he shouted.

Yun Ho's mother closed her eyes and did not speak for a long time. Then she finally said, "Take your marriage money and go to the cattle market tomorrow."

Stars still gleamed palely in the sky of dawn when Yun Ho crossed the hill. He repeated his words, "I will straighten out those big nostrils of his, and bring his chin down. How does it happen in this world that an ugly man has a lovely daughter?"

As farmers arrived and tethered their animals to the stakes, Yun Ho studied every bull until a bearded old man led in a heavy-shouldered animal that threw its big head from side to side and pawed the earth. "This is what I want," Yun Ho decided and approached the owner.

"Five thousand," said the old man. Seeing Yun Ho's disappointment, he added, "I could have sold him for less in my own village, but I crossed five hills to sell for what he is worth."

Yun Ho lingered around, knowing he did not have five thousand but not able to make himself buy any other. The more he hung around the animal, the more Yun Ho was impressed with the sharp horn, the large veins in his throat and strong slanted legs.

At noon the bull was still not sold. The bearded old man asked Yun Ho, "Boy, will you stay with my animal? I will step out to buy a bowl of wine." Then he walked to a nearby wine seller to join several other men who sat crouched, sipping wine.

Running his hand over the mass of muscle along the spine, he felt great strength in the bull. Only now did he admit to himself the extent of his vengeful dreams. Taking hold of the halter, he pulled on it slightly. The bull bellowed once, disapprovingly.

A contemptuous grunt before him startled Yun Ho. "So you are trying to be a cattleman." There was old Kwang with his bull coming into the market. He seldom sold his bull but only amused himself bringing his bull to the fair and telling loudly that his bull was the best.

"How much did you pay for this poor creature?" he asked.

Yun Ho, his lips tight in anger, wouldn't even nod to this bull braggart.

"Don't you recognize your village elder?" Kwang stuck out his bulging stomach importantly. "You should have waited till the sundown when the owner wanted to save himself the trouble of taking home this miserable creature," he said and strode on leading his bull.

Glaring after him angrily, Yun Ho shouted, "Not for half a price, would I buy your miserable animal."

Kwang turned around with his bull and strutted up to Yun Ho. He waved his fat hand, talking, "Should I release this winner of the three village match, your brute would swallow cold and run." He stopped only two or three strides from Yun Ho.

Yun Ho kicked a hunk of cow dung toward him. "Let's fight then. This can win a five-village match." Then he yanked the halter off the bull.

Some called out, "Fight! Fight! Bullfight."

Kwang had already turned his bull loose and stepped back. The two bulls faced each other and their eyes bulged out, shining. Then came the sudden clash of horns. Kwang groaned. More men gathered around the bulls grinding their horns.

The bearded owner of the bull shouted his way through the crowd, "Stop the fight! I brought him to sell, not to fight!" Reaching Yun Ho, he grabbed him by the collar. "You mad rascal, stop the fight!"

Yun Ho shook himself free. "Sell me at four thousand."

"No, five thousand," the bearded man said. He ran to his bull, shouting frantically, "Stop the fight!" He stumbled backward to avoid the hoof of his swirling bull.

Yun Ho pushed him aside. "Get out of the way. You will be gored. Sell me at four thousand."

The bearded man's bull now counted with a charge at his opponent's flank. His bull was shoving Kwang's bull back. He demanded triumphantly, "Five thousand."

As the two glistening bodies moved back and forth, all the crowds yelled to one bull or the other. Kwang ran out, shouting commands and pleaded to his bull. "Charge! Charge!" His bull pushed back forcing the other bull to yield more ground than it had gained.

The bearded man cried to Yun Ho. "Stop the fight." Then he shook Yun Ho by the shoulder, "Pay me five thousand."

Yun Ho broke away from him, asking, "Four thousand?"

"No," the old man raised his voice unhappily. Near the wine woman's mat, his bull, dropping saliva, spread his hind legs to resist the pushing force. The woman swung her ladle toward the bulls, to drive them away. "They are ruining my business. All the drinkers left without paying me."

The bearded man ran up to get closer to his animal but Yun Ho again pushed him aside. "Four thousand."

The old man's face turned to ashen flatness. He stuttered hoarsely, "Have you,—you got all the money with you?"

Yun Ho quickly slipped off his topcoat and threw it toward him. "It's in the pocket." He declared loudly, "The bull is now mine."

He bent his head down as though he were charging, waved his arms like a whip and shouted louder.

As his bull's braced hoofs slipped into the reed mat, a wine jar fell, its white content spilling out. The woman screamed, "Out of my place!" and with her ladle hit the side of Yun Ho's bull.

Startled, the animal freed his horns and leaped away from the mat. The attacking bull was chasing Yun Ho's bull, lowering his horns. The frightened bull spun around, dodged the fierce charge by jumping aside and pulling back his head quickly. Kwang's bull's lunge carried him past his opponent's head. Before he turned his horns to protect his open flank, Yun Ho's bull made a sickening thrust to the belly. Kwang's bull jolted but quickly faced his opponent to stop more butting.

There was a pause. Yun Ho's bull now swirled slowly, lowering his horns to charge, but the other threw up his head and turned to run. The spectators hastily cleared the way.

Yun Ho felt unknown hands lifting him to the broad back of the winning bull. He rode the animal around and around the market, followed by the crowd till he slid off the back to lead him to the shade of a pine nearby to rest.

"Young lad," someone called cheerfully, "come with us. I will treat you to a bowl of wine."

Yun Ho saw a heavy-set man laughing and waving his arm for him to come. Yun Ho did not return his smile but chewed nervously on pine leaves and spat out the bitter taste. Another rugged fellow said,

"Oh, no, not wine for him. He is still an unmarried boy."

Yun Ho's wandering eyes stopped at the wine woman's place where he saw Kwang with other customers. He was sipping wine calmly. He looked neither sad nor even downcast.

The heavy-set man squatted before the wine woman to join the other drinkers, talking happily. "A bull is more clever than a man. When he sees he has no chance he runs away." Some laughed. Kwang did not move from his bent position to look at the joker.

The wine woman stirring a jar's content with her ladle said consolingly, "I am sorry you have lost, but in time the sunny side always becomes the shadow."

Now Kwang spoke loudly for all to hear, "Why do you talk about shadows, woman, when the finest bull in the five villages is marrying into our family." He abruptly got up, holding his head high. "I must hurry to the foolish matchmaker before she talks of Yun Ho to another family."

As he strode away, Yun Ho moved to the bend in the road to watch. Clutching at the bull's shoulder, he said, "I am in the sunny side!" and followed Kwang down the road.

Born in Korea and educated there and in the United States, Kim Yong Ik's short stories appear in prestigious Korean, European and USA periodicals as well as anthologies and his own collections. He has taught at a number of colleges in Korea and is presently teaching in the USA. His short story "From Here You Can See the Moon" was published in SSI No. 31.

"They had been swept away by the changing tide..."

The Changing Tide

BY ALIAS ALI

"WHY shouldn't I feel hurt by the way they've treated me?" Hamid remarked. "If the same thing had happened to you, wouldn't you feel as I do?"

Kassim, the headman of a village in that region, nodded sympathetically.

"Just put yourself in my shoes for a few minutes," Hamid added. "Was it fair for them to do me this way? I've served this State for nearly forty years, and no one, not even a man of greater influence, has done more for the people than I have."

Hamid, who bore several honorary titles for service rendered to his country, pulled off his gold-rimmed glasses. Then he leaned heavily against the gray, thick cushioned sofa, while carefully placing his glasses on the intricately patterned silver tray to his right. He pondered the huge picture on the wall in front of him. Although it looked blurry, he knew it was a picture of himself and Mr. William

Johnsgrave.

He recalled that the picture had been taken not long before independence. With independence had come constitutional changes, and the office of British Adviser to the various states had been abolished, forcing Mr. Johnsgrave to return to England. As a token of their friendship of more than twenty years, Mr. Johnsgrave had invited Hamid to have a picture taken together with him.

Hamid remembered also that Mr. Johnsgrave had dressed in his ceremonial uniform. He wore a tall, white hat decorated with bird feathers at the very top. On his chest were pinned the stars and ribbons given him for meritorious service in the Office of Colonial Affairs. Hanging from the left side of his waist was a sword, reaching down almost to the ground. Hamid was standing to his right, clothed in the traditional Malay headdress and garments worn on special occasions. He also was decorated with medals and ribbons and wore a kris, the serpentine shaped Malay dagger.

This picture was one of Hamid's prize possessions. So he had it mounted in a carved frame painted gold, then hung it in a special place. Every time he looked at the picture he felt nostalgic—those glorious times had gone forever. They had been swept away by the changing tide, which had brought a new constitution and independence.

A bitter smile forced its way across Hamid's lips. "If only Mr. Johnsgrave were still here," he said slowly.

"That would be a different story altogether," Kassim replied.

"It certainly would."

If Mr. Johnsgrave had still been the British Adviser, Hamid could have gone to see him personally, to request that his son be appointed a State government official. Mr. Johnsgrave himself had worked hard to send Azman to England to study law; he had even seen to it that Azman had been given a scholarship by the State. Many people did not agree with the decision. They felt that Azman was not the best qualified person for the scholarship, that others deserved it more. But who would dare to question the decision of a British Adviser?

Azman failed the course. He returned home without receiving the Bachelor of Laws degree. But if Mr. Johnsgrave were still here, there would be no problem at all. Azman's family connections were sufficient to have him appointed a government official. Mr. Johnsgrave had already used his influence to by-pass candidates who perhaps were better qualified. And who would dare question the decision of a British Adviser?

Hamid rubbed his droopy eyes, set beneath a row of thick, bushy eyebrows, now turning white. His prominent, ill-formed nose stood between his soft, flabby cheeks; and rolls of fat were suspended from beneath his long, tapering jaw. He rubbed his hand through his thin layer of white hair before reaching for his glasses. He put them on and sighed deeply.

A middle-aged servant emerged from the kitchen, bringing two cups of coffee, which he ceremoniously placed on a large brass tray immediately in front of the two men. Then he left, bowing as he went, without uttering a word.

"Please drink," Hamid said.

"Oh, yes. Thank you." But Kassim didn't touch his cup, because he noticed that Hamid seemed to be preoccupied.

Hamid picked up a beautifully decorated silver case and opened it.

"Would you like a cigar?" For a moment Kassim appeared a bit puzzled, but finally he took one. Hamid also took out a cigar before closing the silver box and slowly placing it back where it was before. He lit Kassim's cigar, then his own.

After taking a few puffs, Hamid picked up his cup of coffee. "Come on, let's drink our coffee now," he insisted, and he took a sip. Only then did Kassim feel comfortable enough to reach for his own cup.

"That's what's wrong with our people," Hamid affirmed, placing his cup down again; "they soon forget the good things that you've done for them; long years of service mean nothing to them."

"I agree with you. These people think they know it all. Now that they have power, they are unwilling to ask the advice of experienced people like you, Hamid."

"It's not only that they refuse my advise—they simply ignore me completely. In fact, for some time now I've been very much displeased with the people in power, and I'm not at all satisfied with the way they run the government. That's what bothers me the most. Think about it. My son Azman was born and raised in this State; like it or not, he's a native of this State, so it's only fair that he should be given a government post. If they turn down one of their own native sons who has some ability, where will this lead to in the end? In the final analysis it will mean that the more qualified men will leave to seek employment in other states. Then who will be the loser? Our State will. If this is their policy, how will we Malays be benefited at all? They claim to be giving first priority to the Malays."

Kassim nodded in approval.

"Isn't that the way it is, Kassim?" Hamid insisted.

"You're right, Hamid. That's exactly the way things are."

"And you know something else? Azman is not only a native of this State; he's a Malay as well. To be sure, he failed his law examination, but he is still of our own race, and we must give preference to them. Don't you think it's better to employ one of our own people, than to give positions to someone else?"

"Certainly I do."

"Things are difficult nowadays. Our Chief Minister refuses to listen to advice. He wants to act on his own. During the time of the previous Chief Minister, the situation was much more pleasant. He was willing to accept the advice of others, and, if not, he always had to heed the advice of the British Adviser. In those days I was a close friend of Mr. Johnsgrave. You know that yourself. He never refused my advice."

"Have you gone to see the new chairman of the Public Service Commission? Do you know who he is?"

"Zainal."

"Oh, yes."

"I've phoned him, and he's willing to help in whatever way he can. There's no need for me to go visit him personally; a phone call should be sufficient. He knows Azman well. I helped Zainal get his first job as an employee in the land office. He had no experience at that time, but he was crazy about politics. That's how he got his present position."

"It wouldn't be right of him not to help you."

"But the Chief Minister also has a say in the matter, and he doesn't like me, because I've never thought much of him. I know him for sure. He used to go around on a bicycle, selling cloth. You remember him."

"I certainly do." Kassim smiled a bit.

"Yes, he used to ride a bicycle; now he goes around in a Mercedes Benz. Today he sits in a car with government flags on it; before that he had never even been near the palace. But he's a politician, and they can do anything. These days, if you want to climb the ladder fast, just enter politics. Even a cloth seller can become the Chief Minister!"

"Quick to rise; quick to fall."

Hamid laughed, and his chair shook a bit. He stared blankly at one corner of the room, then he stole a glance at the pair of elephant tusks displayed on the wall.

"He's really upset with me," Hamid went on to say. "Sometime ago he came here, requesting help for his party. They wanted to demand independence and to hold public elections. But how could I do anything for them? I was tied up with the government at that time, and a member of Exco as well. Besides, Mr. Johnsgrave himself advised me not to get involved, because, according to him, all political moves in those days were directed against the British. He was right. Just as soon as we got our independence, qualified people like him lost their positions."

Hamid shook the ashes from his cigar into a silver ashtray. Then he sipped his coffee again. Kassim also took another sip of his coffee.

Hatijah started out of the house. She was an ample, buxom woman, and the loose fitting, but stylish dress she wore made her rotund body appear even broader. Hatijah was fiftyish, some five years younger than her husband. Rows of gold bangles ornamented her arms, an enormous gold necklace hung from her neck, and she wore a pair of sparkling diamond earrings.

"Have you been here long?" she asked with a smile.

"Not very long," Kassim replied, making an attempt to rise from his chair.

Hamid just rolled his cigar around between his fingers, without moving from his seat.

"How is everyone at home?"

"Fine. Everyone is just fine."

"Why didn't you bring your wife along with you?"

Kassim smiled, as though to ask her apologies.

"She's too busy with all the children. You know, the older you get, the more grandchildren you have."

Hatijah laughed.

Hamid grinned.

"It's been a long time since you've come by for a visit," Hatijah remarked. "What have you been doing with yourself lately?"

"Err...Please forgive me. Actually I've planned for some while to drop by, and just as soon as I heard that Azman had returned from England, I came right on over. I wanted very much to see him, but I find he's not at home."

"Since his return yesterday he's not spent much time at home. Last night Bendahara gave a party in his house to celebrate Azman's homecoming. I understand there is also to be a dinner in his honor tonight. He's done nothing but have a good time since returning. I urged him to make a visit to the palace, but he said he didn't have time. You know Azman; he's hardheaded."

"We were talking about Azman when you came in," Kassim indicated. "I'm sorry to hear what has happened. He certainly deserves a position in the State Government."

"The Chief Minister is a little difficult," Hatijah replied, glancing over at her husband.

"Not a little difficult—very difficult," Hamid emphasized.

Kassim shook his head, then remarked, "It's not easy to deal with our people. I found it easier to work with the Europeans."

"I agree with you absolutely," Hamid said immediately. "Absolutely. It was much easier to get along with the Europeans. They were not so tempermental."

"The Europeans recognized good breeding," Hatijah added. "Our people are hard to get along with, to say the least."

Hamid grunted, "That's exactly why our State administration is in such a mess."

"If that's the way things are, our State could be in for some real trouble," Kassim stressed.

"Mr. Johnsgrave himself once told me," Hamid added, "if things are not handled properly, our State could get into serious difficulties. Under the British administration all matters were properly taken care of. But now? Just see for yourself. Our treasury is constantly short of funds and our budget is always running a deficit, because we are producing less and less. This is every bit the fault of our present administration. During the British times we were never short of funds; the British were careful how they spent the money. But now? Those in charge of our finances spend the money recklessly. They are building roads, mosques, clinics, and a thousand other things, claiming it is all for the betterment of our people. But what has it all come to? Our treasury is so low on funds that we cannot pay our employees. The next thing you know they will have to borrow money from the Federal Government. Tens of millions of dollars. And how will they ever pay that back? Our State Government will be in pawn to the Federal Government."

Kassim shook his head once more.

"The situation is really bad when they are unwilling to accept advice," Hatijah interjected. "They refuse to come to men like my husband for advice. They think they're smart, that they know all there is to know. That's why my husband and others like him have been shoved into the background. The present administration cares nothing about us. We're no longer even invited to the formal State functions."

"It's gone that far?" Kassim replied with a show of surprise.

"Yes it has. For two or three years now we've not been invited to those functions, whether in the home of the Chief Minister or in the palace itself. I was told that there was a dinner given at the palace last night in honor of a minister of the Federal Government. But we weren't invited. Instead they invited some of the people from the villages, those people they call village leaders. Half of them know nothing of palace protocol. They have never been in the palace before in their lives; how could they know? I've heard a lot of stories about things that have taken place there. Palace protocol is not easy to master. You know that yourself, Kassim, you've been to the palace before."

"How true it is. How true." Kassim chimed in.

"Let me tell you something that happened," Hamid said with a grin. "Some of the village leaders actually came to the palace wearing a kris."

"My God!" Kassim exclaimed. "That's the worst possible breach of palace etiquette."

"Certainly. But fortunately one of the palace officials noticed them and had the men leave their krises with him. Otherwise, who knows what might have happened?" Hamid snickered.

"That isn't all either," Hatijah continued. "Some of them didn't even know how to use a spoon and fork."

"They didn't know how to eat with a spoon and fork?"

"No. I heard this myself from one of the palace officials. Not only that. Some of them didn't know the proper way to drink tea. Why they actually dipped cookies in their tea."

"At the palace?"

"Yes, at the palace!"

"Oh God!" Kassim replied, striking himself on the forehead.

"Isn't that embarrassing?"

"Embarrassing and disgraceful!" Kassim shook his head.

"Please don't get involved with those people," Hamid pleaded.

"I certainly won't," Kassim quickly replied. "No, I'll never do that. They're constantly urging me to join their party, but I refuse to do so. I cooperate with them and work as hard as I can in projects that benefit my village, but I would never get involved in their politics. Never!"

"Good. If you did, you would become just like them."

"I'm no politician."

"Don't get involved, Kassim. Don't. If I had wanted to go into politics, I could have done so a long time ago. Perhaps by now I would have been a minister in the Federal Government, if I had joined their party before independence." Then he laughed.

Kassim laughed with him.

"Why, Kassim, if you had gone into politics from the first, you would surely be an honored member of Parliament by now."

They laughed again.

"People say politics is a dirty game," Hamid went on to comment.

A car stopped in front of the house. Azman jumped out and talked for a few minutes with someone inside the car. Then the car sped away, and Hamid noticed the crest above the license plate, indicating the owner was a member of the State Legislature. When Azman entered the house, Hamid looked at him with deep concern.

The young man, tall and thin with ruffled hair, shook hands with Kassim. They began talking about one thing and another, while Hamid kept wondering about the car with the crest on it. He wanted to ask his son who it was that had brought him home, but the question remained unasked.

"Azman, I was very sorry to hear what happened," Kassim said.

"Sorry?" Azman asked in amazement.

"Yes. I felt you should have been given a position in the State Government."

Azman smiled. He glanced over at his father, then at his mother. "I never dreamed of that," he said, conscious that his parents were staring at him.

"What are your plans for the future?"

"I've entered politics."

"Politics?" his father blurted out in a high pitched voice.

"Yes," the young man answered; then he got up and went out.

Hamid, Kassim, and Hatijah just looked at one another.

At that moment Hamid suddenly realized that he was old, that for him life's sunset was approaching. Not only was he no longer influential in government circles, but he was unable even to control his own son's way of thinking.

Hamid's cigar was now too short to smoke; the fire had almost died out.

 *Alias Ali was born in 1933 in Kuala Trengganu. He resigned as General News Editor of the Malaysian National News Agency in 1978 to run in the General Election and won the parliamentary seat of Ulu Trengganu. He has published several novels and collections of short stories. He also writes poetry, essays and dramas.*

"And now he has been there for three days,
unable to fathom the event."

The Waterfall

BY BRUNO SCHWEBEL

WHEN the old man was born, nearby, it was already there. In its waters his children had their first bath, and in its ponds his wife washed the rags which served as their diapers. And later, when she died, the waterfall was still there. He could remember it from his infancy without any great changes. Of course, during the rains it carried more water, and in the dry season, a little less; but the flow miraculously prevailed.

The waterfall wasn't high, but it was wide; languid and calming. Powerful. The first descent, a majestic unfolding of curtains of water, gave to the largest pool. More rivulets followed, offspring of the main current, which dropped to different levels, forming eddies and little turquoise ponds ideal for romping. Clouds of water nebulized by the breezes vibrated in a strange song, accompanied by the crazy rhythms of little rils of foam which wove among the rocks: a symphony of life, paced by the incessant pounding of those masses which fell and fell, which rose in rebellion, only to drop once again and finally join the torrent which was tamed further on, forming at last only a few waves of protest and some reluctant whirlpools. Since he was old enough to reason, he had listened to the same litany, the same roar; and downriver, to the same murmurs.

But now there is silence. Three days have passed since the waterfall died; the old man is still dumbfounded by the sight of this bare skull. Yes, it is an enormous skull, strange, its forehead that huge boulder which protrudes above. The sockets of its eyes are those caverns, still humid, whose depths reflect opaque, lifeless lights.

The old fellow gazes, tired. So tired, he gazes at those strange caves which in his entire life he has never seen; they have always been covered by thick veils of water. But there was one, the one at the bottom. Finding their way in through the cascade was ever a favorite adventure of the boys. "Look, look! A cave! Let's go in!"

At the end of a day, when everyone was gone and the waterfall remained alone with the sunset and with the old fellow, the swallows began to swoop back and forth. Coming and going. Swooping...coming...going...What a din! Parakeets, hummingbirds, starlings—the whole flock in the daily twilight scandal, supervised from above by the hawk who sways attentively, dangling from the sunset. And now where are they? They are still there, yes, but the hubbub is changed; confused.

And that, now, is how the old man feels. He has been there for three days, on his chair, his eyes fixed on the massive skeleton. That lifeless monster, with its sad trickles where before there were streams; with its dry, cracked remains where before plants burst through, saturated with juices and green; with mud where before water quivered in the breezes of the cascade.

One day, years ago, he watched his children leaping over the ponds. The youngest was so fearful! How well the old man remembers it now. As he sits there, parts of his life pass through his mind over and over; other images obstinately don't appear at all. But each and every one of his children's experiences related to that waterfall now acquires a vivid clarity. That first jump over the pool filled the youngest equally with fear and pride. Of course! It was his big step into life itself. He grew strong and straight. It's he who now works on the ranch near the Rio Verde.

Three days have passed since the electric company diverted the stream of the waterfall to feed a new hydroelectric plant, which in turn will regenerate life in its own way. The old fellow paid no attention to the warnings. When his daughter-in-law Juanela told him, he answered that he was going to dry some rattan to repair the chairs. His mind simply refused to take it in. And now he has been there for three days, unable to fathom the event. Without even trying to. The dead waterfall is reflected in his now flaccid face, a life at end. At times he thinks he hears again the voices of the visitors who used to come to the falls in loud anticipation. He images himself once more blinded by the reflections of the sunset on the water, laughing at the kids' splashing, watching the rainbow which emerges from the big bobo tree and which curves down to the bend of the river, where on weekends the crayfish would hide, frightened away by the noise. "A peso of oranges, Grandpa"..."Look at the fish!" The recollection of the sun on the water contracts his vision and warms his soul. And bitterness chills it.

Three days have passed since the old man began to die, at the side of the waterfall which saw him live, that cascade which was the irrefutable presence of his God. Intuitively he understood the work of the Creator in that waterfall, he understood that it signified the flow of life itself, perennial, immortal. And for that reason, precisely for that reason, he is sitting there now, just sitting, without understanding. Gone. Hypnotized by this tremendous event. His mind wanders, scanning the past—"Hey, old man, how much for a sugar cane?" "Let's go fish for turtles, Grandpa!"—searching desperately for some support, some familiar voice, friendly smiles, in the nearness of the unknown, the total end.

Juanela came on Sundays, setting up early in the morning for the visitors who would buy quesadillas and snacks. To sell more, she even let the boys tease. She was pretty, Juanela. "Is that your daughter, old man?" "How's the baby, Juanela?" Oh, she was a fine girl, Juanela. She always found time to sweep, to pick guavas, or to weed a patch of the garden. It was a small garden, constantly watered by the cascade, leafy and tropical, generous, splendid, in it a few shacks, the old man's home. A man alone for years because his children preferred the villages and his wife had been gone since he planted the lemon tree. He was just able to live on his pay from the government for tending the swimming hole, and from the stand with its little mounds of fruit, pyramids of sugar cane, soft drinks, cigarettes, cookies, and candies for Sunday excursionists.

But now it's all over.

Three days have passed since the water abruptly lessened. The old fellow was shelving some boxes when the sudden quiet, the absence of that constant and eternal percussion, made him turn. The silence was born. He didn't even scratch his head, as was his custom. He just sat down very slowly to watch. It was like seeing someone beloved die from bleeding. Now only the gurgling of agonizing rills is left, when yesterday something still flowed between those rocks. How many times—thousands, maybe—did he slide from above, to fall happily into the big swimming hole? "Come on, Lencho, don't be a sissy! Jump!" the voices echo. He always had to shout because the waterfall would not be dominated. Shiny little bodies would climb and climb, and they would climb up, again and again, to dive from the rock, to dive and to dive again, to slide, to tumble down, splatter, splash, and shout; day after day.

But now the voices are dominated by the silence which radiates from the enormous skull, absorbed by those huge toothless hollows. An unfamiliar stench replaces last week's fragrances. The sun, yesterday a bestower of life, today overpowering and mortal, exterminates the dying. Today, it's a dry and suffocating heat, where yesterday fresh breezes carried their cargo of pulverized waterfall. Repugnant slime, oozing mire, and cracked mud; dry, blinding, burning stones. Dead fish. Graveyard.

The old man is part of it all. Immobile, no longer on his chair, he has slipped. Leaning on a large rock, he blinks slowly, very slowly, his vision clouded, his feet covered with ants and his skin with mosquitoes, in a banquet of dying.

Now it is all over. No longer will people come. Never. Soon it will all be wilderness again. This Sunday Juanela will arrive with her tortilla dough, lard and ice; and afterwards, some relative will come to take everything away.

On the back of a pickup will go the many, but so few, belongings of all of one life.

A refugee from Nazi Austria, Bruno Schwebel arrived in Mexico in 1942. He is an author, electronic engineer, painter and actor. For the last 10 years he has been writing short stories in Spanish. Currently, he is at work on a new collection of short stories and a novel. "The Waterfall" was translated from Spanish by the author and Joan Brodovsky, his wife.

"...he is making me seem an old man who cannot remember what he has seen."

The Witness Man

BY VINCENT O'SULLIVAN

WHILE Clem ate his sardines and toast he also fed the cat, handing down crusts dipped in the oil at the bottom of the tin. "You old thing," he said, "you'd scoff on until you burst, wouldn't you, eh?" He scraped at the corner of the tin with his fork and tipped the flakes of fish, as well as what oil remained, onto his own plate. Nan would have had something to say about that now, wouldn't she, using the same plate for himself and puss? The cat hummed like a small engine as it rubbed against his trousers, then raised itself to tap at the plate with its paw before it reached the cork matting under the table. The elderly man ran his fingers in the thick fur at the animal's neck. There used to be a collar there but it had worn thin with the years and the randy old blighter had probably lost it in a fight. He might be twelve years old but he still came in some mornings with scratches on his face, or a chunk torn out of his ear. "Real old soldier, aren't you?" Clem told him. The cat licked the oil from the plate and moved away from the old man's hand. He's a cool one, Clem thought. Wouldn't miss me for a second as long as someone was giving him his tucker.

It amused him to think of how he sometimes waited for the cat to come in and the darned old thing didn't give a damn one way or the other about him. Nan used to tell him he was a softie about it, about cats, about everything. They almost rowed just after the war when her brother had put up with them for what at first was meant to be a fortnight but lengthened out into four months. "You can't turf him out like that," Clem said. "We don't know what he's had to put up with, do we?" Dear old Nan, she couldn't see softness had nothing to do with it, it was what you owed a bloke. Yet if it was sentimental you were talking about, well Nan was the one there, all right. She'd cry up at the pictures at the Britannia on a Saturday night even when the story had a happy ending. Her favorites were the ones with soldiers saying good-bye to girls on bridges, or the women waiting and looking up while squadrons flew away above them, and you knew by the music that was that. And he'd say to Nan "It's only a picture, remember." She would tuck her hand in the pocket of the gaberdine he used to wear then and he'd squeeze it tight in his own as they crossed at the Three Lamps then took their time walking down St. Mary's Road. The light always seemed softer, the night more fresh or something, when you had just come out from the pictures. And walking round was safe as a church in those days. You'd see a group of young fellows walking towards you and you'd never think of crossing over, not even if they were smart alecking about or drinking from bottles. And now here we were, Clem thought, no wars or anything to see people off, and you thought twice about going up the road once it was dark. The other day he heard two women talking about it on the steps of Leys Institute. One of them was saying "His head was caved in like a pumpkin or something."

"They must have been after his money, were they?"

"Like hell they were. It was just for the fun of it."

Clem picked up the plate and ran it under the hot tap. He put out his hand to stroke the cat again but the old beggar raised itself from the chair it was lying on, and hopped down to avoid him. "All right," Clem told it, "I'm not going to maul you." He opened the door and stood there above the cat for a moment, looking across the small sloping lawn with its one tree, and on down the sharp fall of the street towards the motorway, the sea, the arc of the harbor bridge. Must be getting on for twenty years since that was built, musn't it? Since he and Nan used to sit out here in the late afternoons. They had watched the whole thing, from when the bulldozers first came in and started ripping up the beach beneath the park until the two steel arms narrowed the space between them, and at last they met like that, in that arch he liked to look at, the lovely easy line that took the traffic up and flowed down the other side. And across the gray web of the bridge he could still make out the Chelsea sugar works, his eyes weren't doing too bad were they? Before the bridge was even talked about Nan needed her glasses to make things out on the other side. He looked across now to the clutter of buildings against the blue bush on the hill around them. He wouldn't mind a tanner for every time he'd crossed that stretch of water.

The first day on the job over there one of the lads called him colonel because of his neat clipped moustache. The name had stuck with him, right until he retired. He never let on that it covered a scar from when he was a boy, from the day the old man pushed him out of the way in the shop and he'd caught his face on an opened biscuit tin.

"Here's the colonel," one of them called out when he came into the lunchroom. "Left the bloody horse outside, have we?" The clerks weren't the most popular blokes at the best of times, but Clem made out all right. The thing was you didn't try to have them on in return, that was the answer. Come at that boy and you were a goner. They'd never let up if they got a rise out of you. There was one bloke there, for instance, he used to read the Bible at lunch time and he would answer them with quotes, this mild almost silly smile on his face even when they asked him which way the missus liked it, talked to him like that. Or another one, an Italian. They called him Mussolini Arseholes anyway because they never gave him a break. So when Clem had first turned up they naturally worked on him for a bit and then they let up, there wasn't enough sport in it. "Once they know they can't get at you the penny drops soon enough." He had explained that to Nan soon after he started there, when someone had filled with sugar the leather bag that he carried his lunch and the odd book in. She was in tears about the mess it made and he had tried to tell her, "Look, they're always doing someone over. Don't create about it and they'll lay off."

"They sound like animals," Nan said.

"They're no worse than anywhere else," Clem defended them.

Funny how those days come back to him more strongly since the trouble began. It had stirred the past up, Clem thought, like shoving a stick into a swarm of bees. When he looked across now to the distant works he could smell again that hot sweetness he took months to get used to; and the odor of the sea, when he had leaned over the side of the ferry and picked out their house, and Nan was a speck on the veranda with a tea towel waving in her hand. Even the smell of their bedroom—that came back too some of these nights. Nan's own smell and her way of clutching at his shoulder when they were man and wife together. As if I'm not a bit past that, Clem thought, as if with the old ticker and all he shouldn't be taking life pretty quietly, instead of waking with the old memories disturbing him. Then thinking of that led him on to other things and sometimes it was hours before he slept again, the old sadnesses about Nan's illness and even years before that, when they still thought they might have a family.

The cat had returned from scratching beneath the tree. "We can't do much about it now, eh boy?" Clem said. "Just two old cobbers getting along quite nicely." This time the cat allowed Clem to finger the deep soft fur of his chest. Right under the doubled front leg he could feel the cat's heart going nineteen to the dozen, although the blighter just lay there, rolling on its side.

Clem hadn't spoken to a policeman since before the war. The last time was at the safety zone in front of Court's in Queen Street, the night the Labour Party won its second election. Earlier that night he and Nan were sitting over their tea, listening to the wireless and talking about how it had been only ten years ago say, what a different world it was now. The way Nan for instance had to call people Sir or Madam when she opened the door of the house in Mountain Road. The lawyer she worked for gave her a fiver at Christmas and a glass of sherry and then got her against the fireplace, his hand trying to go up under her dress and even while he was doing that Nan was saying

Sir to him. "Don't be silly, sir," she kept telling him. She knew if she lost that job there wouldn't be another and Clem had been laid off only a few weeks before. She hadn't mentioned it to him for another two years, until he was working again and she was off sick herself, sick for the first time. She was sitting up in bed reading the paper and saw the name of the people she used to work for.

"See he's dead," Nan said.

"Someone we know?"

"That poor old sod who tried to handle me that Christmas." She told Clem the story like it was a joke. At first he thought By Christ I wish he was still alive and I'd fix with him all right, but then he was angry with Nan. She said "Oh, don't go on about it. I hated it more than anything in my life."

"But you felt sorry for him didn't you?" Clem insisted.

Nan had shrugged at him as if it didn't matter. "Well I suppose I did." And that was in Clem's mind as they sat there the night of the election. It had been raining earlier and the earth outside the opened window smelled alive and wet. The leaves of the lemon tree near the clothesline glittered when he moved the curtain back and looked out at the yard. He was thinking of Nan pushed up against the carved mantelpiece she had told him about, that the old bitch at the house used to make her clean with a special tiny brush. Well the bugger was dead now and he supposed it didn't matter. But he thought of how he had got away with it because of his money and how Nan used to get up early and walk to Epsom sometimes before the first tram, to be there when they had special visitors staying and they wanted their breakfast early. He looked out at the November sky above the house next door. "By God they'll never come at that again," Clem said.

Why didn't they walk down town? Nan asked him. They might as well get the excitement of it when Savage got back in. Everybody said "Savage" in Ponsonby, rather than "Labour" because you were talking about the same thing, about the ordinary people who wouldn't be kicked round any more, about better things than money to judge things by. Clem had never been that shook on crowds yet he didn't want to miss this one, he was glad Nan had suggested it. So they walked from their cottage on the corner to the end of the

Convent grounds, then down the little lane to Jacob's Ladder. Who on earth had called it that? Nan used to say. And Clem would tell her "Those nuns, don't you reckon?" They owned half the land between here and the Lamps, they gave the streets those saints' names and the Bishop's Palace still rose up among the workers' houses like something in a history book, turret and all. Anyway, it seemed a good name for that long flight of steps. There were a hundred of them, he supposed, dropping steeply down, close to the face of the yellowish clay cliff. At the bottom you could pick your way round the rocks or you could walk the other way, to the broad park with the tall oaks all round it. And fifteen minutes after that you could be in the middle of the city. "It's mad this, you know," he said to Nan. They had turned to the left at the bottom as they always did, because Nan couldn't pass the water without dabbling in it.

"What is?" she said.

"Living like we do in the center of Auckland nearly, the tram along the road and that, and here we go picking our way round rocks like there wasn't any other way." Nan laughed and looked out over the harbor, across the stretch of mud where the tide had fallen back, "I love that smell, don't you Clem?" She stood awkwardly on a slab of soft crumbly rock. He thought how she loved the beach yet she never looked quite at home away from streets and kitchens and things, she looked as though she would lose her balance any minute and tumble forward. But God she looked lovely standing there all the same. She wore her coat with the fringe of imitation fur at the cuffs and a hat that came right down over her ears. It was nearly dark by now and he looked at her raised above the little beach, the lights over the other side twinkling away behind her, across the water that was now lighter for some reason than the sky. "Come on," he said. They had gone across the park with leaves freshly out on those great trees and the racket from the birds, a city of birds just settling down. And funnily enough Clem had forgotten the rest, wasn't that just the oddest thing? Not a thing about the crowd in front of the newspaper office or the cheering when the results went up like the results on a totalizator or the noise when they saw how they had put Savage back with the biggest lead in the country. He had forgotten those things although he had talked about them dozens of times and not so long ago there was a display of pictures of that night up at the Institute. The pictures were in a glass case and there were political books with their pages held back like birds' wings and Clem had thought Well it's just about like that now, it's all pretty near museum stuff for what it matters any more. He had watched while a couple of young women came up and glanced at the photos then turned away, their faces as blank as though they had looked at a wall. And the once or twice he had talked about those days to clever young people he had felt it was lost nearly as much as it was with those two women. Their interest in those days, the words they used, the way they had wanted him to say it or something, just didn't hang together. "You must remember something about that night, you must have sensed its significance?" one of them had pressed him. He had sat there in his grubby enough clothes for a clever young bloke, he had a notebook on his knee and it was like Clem had to answer charges. "Well I don't," Clem had said, "I don't remember a thing, I wish I could help you some more." He was blowed if he was going to say about Nan there standing on the rock when the sky was almost dark but the sea was silvery like an old mirror, or about the poor devil they'd seen after all the excitement was over outside the *Star* office, and they came on this other crowd gathering round the safety zone at Court's. He and Nan were suddenly among the closest to the low concrete platform. A tram had stopped halfway across the intersecting streets and they saw the conductor jump down, his bag jolting in front of him and the loose change jangling as he jumped. The conductor ran back towards them and picked up something from beside the shining grooves of the rails. At the same time, as though from the one pair of eyes, he and Nan had noticed the well-dressed man who was sitting on the safety zone, one leg across the other, his knee supporting the ankle that he held in both hands. When the conductor stooped down he picked up a boot with a foot inside it. He carried the boot in both his own hands and knelt down beside the man, as though he were a salesman showing it to a customer. The man looked at him without speaking. Clem remembered how there was no expression of pain on the youngish, surprised face. Then someone broke from the crowd of watchers and started shouting, Get the ambulance, will you. A couple of women screamed too and Nan had pressed against him, her hand holding onto his. And before two policemen came running and thrusting through the crowd Clem watched the black stain spreading on the knee of the man's gray flannel trousers. With a kind of careful modesty the man's efforts now seemed to be to protect his wound from those who watched him. Both his hands were cupped over his ankle, he hardly moved his head when the conductor put the foot beside him on the platform. Clem heard the conductor say "I don't know what the hell I'm supposed to do." But he kept kneeling beside the man and put his arm across his shoulders. Even as he watched Clem was thinking why do I notice such unimportant things when a man is bleeding to death? For he saw how the street lights shivered down the leather strap across the conductor's back, and the way the boot was standing by itself, a flat lid of shadow across the top, and so highly polished there was a pip of light winking on its toecap.

That was when Clem had last spoken to a policeman. Because he and Nan were at the front of the crowd it was assumed that they had seen it all. "But we didn't even notice the tram until it stopped," he said. "Until we saw the conductor getting off."

"We'll still need your names," the policeman said. That was a few minutes or so later, after the chap had been off in an ambulance and the driver had lifted up the foot and placed it inside, beside the stretcher, with a towel draped over it. That long ago and Clem had never really spoken to a cop since, not like that, not about questions and times and where exactly he stood. Now this young rooster who looked as if he still didn't know what a razor was had flicked his book open while they sat at the kitchen table. When this boy policeman said "Where would you like to begin then, eh?" he suddenly saw that other book opening, all those years ago, the hand slowly writing their address down while the crowd still milled round.

"I'd better begin when the girl first went past me," Clem said. "Is that the bit you want to know about?"

The policeman said "I want to hear about all of it. Sooner or later it'll have to come out in court, won't it?"

They asked him the same questions over and over. How could he be certain about the time? Surely his sight must be extraordinary for an elderly gentleman? And his observation, too. Wasn't that out of the ordinary?

"I can't say what ordinary is," Clem said. "I can only talk about what I saw for myself. I've always had good eyesight so I just sort of take things in."

"You see what a perceptive witness we're dealing with, my lord," the police lawyer said when the business had got that far, when Clem stood with both his hands resting on the polished wooden ledge in front of him. He felt that the man didn't like him, it was not just a matter of doing his job. He wanted to trap him somehow, he was trying to say one way and then another that because Clem was old they could hardly expect him to get things correct. He asked him questions about what work he had done before he retired, then he made it all seem so unimportant, being a tally clerk for most of his life, working in the Corso store for the last few years. Clem was annoyed with himself when he said "My wife was very ill for a long time then. I had to get a job where I could come and go more easily." The lawyer just looked at him when he said that and he was left standing there, as though he had said something foolish. Clem had raised his hand and passed it across his neatly clipped moustache and a voice from beneath him told him he could step down. As he turned and left the box he knew he was right about it, knew in the way you sometimes do by intuition, that the lawyer had disliked him because of his moustache, because of his careful answers. He wasn't dumb and senile the way the lawyer wanted him to be, that was what the pleased-with-himself bastard had been hinting at, wasn't it, with his shrugs and hitching at the folds of his gown?

Why on earth would he be inaccurate about it? Clem thought. It wasn't properly dark anyway, there were lights half way up the steps as well as directly above where he had been standing. There was nothing so extraordinary about noticing two figures who stood at one of the landings halfway down, a man and a woman arguing together. He had seen the man's high fuzzed hair and he had thought why do girls go round with them in the first place? If it came to that he had never seen what men saw in dark women either, all that nonsense you used to hear after the War from blokes who had been up in the islands or over in Egypt or wherever, and they'd say you couldn't beat them, there wasn't a woman back home who could touch them when it came to the dinkum thing. Nan laughed when they spoke about it, there was nothing he couldn't talk to her about then. "I bet the Japs'd be saying the same things about us, if they'd ever got here," she said. "You don't have to know much about men to know that one, Clem."

The dark man had put out his hand and rested it on the girl's arm. Her head tilted back as though she was trying to look straight up at the stars, because Clem saw the whiteness of her throat before she tried to break free from the man who held her by the wrist, who tried to move towards and over her. She strained away from him and was drawn back again. Clem saw the girl's own hand come up slowly as if she intended stroking the man's face. Then he heard the man call out, he shouted at her obscenely as she lunged away from him, falling against the steps as he freed her wrist. She scrambled up and then began running up the steps to where Clem stood back against the railing at the top to let her pass. Her face was raised towards him. When she saw him she stopped running and walked past him at a normal pace. (How do you know what a *normal pace* is for a young lady?" the lawyer smiled.) She was breathing heavily and her eyes turned again to look at him, but she said nothing as she went by. When she was further along the alley towards the street she began to run again, a clopping awkward run, her wooden-heeled shoes loud against the surface of the path.

"You're quite sure she didn't speak to you?" both the lawyers in due course would ask him, as the policeman had that next morning when Clem answered the knock on the glass panel in the front door. *What did you see?* I saw a dark man about thirty talking to a young woman who was twenty say, or twenty-five. *How long did you watch them?* It wasn't so much watching as that they just stayed half-way down the steps while I was standing at the top. It is where I stand most evenings if the weather's fine. I like the view from there over the yacht harbor and I used to stand there with my wife. *Would you say you saw anything unusual occur?* I saw a man and girl talking and then arguing, I saw them struggle with each other for a little and move as if to make up and then the woman must have scarred the man's face, although at the time I thought she was touching his face

and not scratching it. I just saw what men and women have been doing forever, I suppose. The lawyer turned and smiled at the jury when he said that too. And on the questioning went on and on, over and over. *You didn't realize something more serious was taking place?* I thought both the man and the girl were serious. *We mean did you realize it was something criminal?* No, Clem said to the policeman, No sir, to both the lawyers who asked him that as well. And when they asked him what did he notice about the girl he said he noticed she ran up the steps, he guessed she simply wanted to get away from the man. The man called her bitch several times as she ran away from him. He continued to shout words of that kind and probably in another language also, even after she had crossed the road and was gone. She wore something, a medallion or cross or a locket, around her throat. It glinted in the light and it jumped up and down in front of her as she ran. Clem went over most of what he had said as he sat after his tea, and thought about the court. It was all so clear in his mind but he hadn't been able to get the feel of it through, had he? Not so they saw it as he did. She had simply run away from the man and there was no terror in it, as the smart lawyer wanted him to agree, no fear nor panic as she ran up the steps, her breasts moving inside the tight jersey thing she was wearing, and the chain rose and fell at every step she took. *She looked at the witness?* Not directly but her eyes sort of slid across, they were shining but there were no tears either, that was another thing the lawyer had wanted him to say. She was no more than a few feet from him, how could he be wrong? The down on her neck beneath the close cropped hair was touched with light, he could see that even, that's how close he was. She couldn't have been crying without his noticing it. Because later it was so obvious the man was.

But you didn't wait for the accused to walk up the steps? I was back near the wall where the convent playing courts are, when I heard the man behind me. He was wearing sandshoes so I didn't know until he was nearly right beside me. Then when I turned I looked straight into his face. No, he did not speak to me, no, I don't think he even saw me. And the lawyer said to him then, You thought? Shall we confine ourselves to what you *know?* So Clem had said nothing. He felt his hands slip against the wooden edge of the witness box and the flush, the warmth, rise at the back of his neck. He is wanting me to lose the thread of what I have to say, he is making me seem an old man who cannot remember what he has seen.

There was no way of telling the court so they might see it as clearly as he had himself, the broad dark face with tears streaming across it, glazing in the light from the lamppost on the other side of the street. Not that, nor the smear of sweat and tears and snot that spread on his upper lip and and at the corners of his nose, the three seeping lines dragged across one cheek by the girl's scarlet nails. For they were scarlet when he looked at her hands in court, when he heard her say that she marked the man in self-defense. "It's when I scratched him like that he let me go. Up till then he was saying he would do it again. He would drag me back to the side of the steps where he had done it before." The court was shown a gray plastic raincoat the accused had been carrying when he passed Clem, although the older man did not remember seeing it. *This,* the lawyer said. He held up the coat for them to see. It was creased and smeared with mud, and the prosecutor asked might he draw their attention to certain other stains?

Clem's confusion grew as the day moved on, as he heard others stand in the box and the judge warn them to take their words and weigh them, and for a moment he saw that too in his mind, the ancient image of scales in perfect balance, then one pan tipping slightly, those could be his words that made it tip. He looked carefully at the girl when her own turn came to be questioned. She answered very clearly in a voice he nevertheless leaned forward to hear. And then the man. He spoke so quietly Clem missed some of what was said. Twice the judge halted him to say that he must speak up. The second time he instructed him to look up as well, there was no point mumbling down at his chest, the court was over here. There was another Islander who stood not far from him, who sometimes translated phrases for him when he was not sure of what was asked. And the translator spoke to the court when the man once answered at length in his own language. That was the one time he seemed confident. He raised his head and gestured with one hand, he turned to where the girl sat and turned again towards the

judge, coming back to English as he said "You listen to him again."
He pointed to where Clem sat. "You ask him, you ask the witness
man." The lawyer smiled and said "But we already have. Surely you
must have heard him?" The man's face became passive again, he
looked down at his hands, one laid across the other on the railing in
front of him. *The jigsaw,* the lawyer said. He stood in front of the
jury. *You must piece it together.*

So the court put together its picture. Its figures were the man and
the girl who worked together in Fanshawe Street. They cleaned
offices after most of the staff went home. They had worked together
for three months, and sometimes, because they lived in Ponsonby,
they walked home together. The girl said Well it was natural wasn't
it, she felt safer when he walked with her. If she was by herself she
would never think of taking that short cut up the steps, she would go
home by bus. Her mother said yes, that was true, her employer said
she was a good worker, the lawyer read a letter that told how last
year she gave a month of her time collecting for Telethon. And the
girl herself had told them how once or twice after work the man had
wanted to kiss her. The girl laughed and told him don't be silly, he
was married wasn't he? And then he had begun to get heavy.

Heavy? the judge queried. And she answered "Just pushing his
luck a bit."

That night, then? she was prompted. That night when they were
on the asphalt pathway between the motorway and the steps, the
man had dragged her from the path, between the clumps of toi-toi.
The traffic sped past them twenty yards away and no one else had
walked along the path. He had grabbed at her and struggled at her
clothes. The girl told them in that same clear voice how he had put
one foot behind her leg and forced her back onto the coat he threw
down beneath them. And how could she call out when she knew no
one was round? That he carried a knife? Then the court was shown
that as well, a dull horn-handled pocket knife. *He carried this,* the
lawyer said. He passed the knife to the foreman of the jury. Some of
them touched its edge with their thumbs and turned it over in their
palms before passing it on. But he had not taken it out, the other
lawyer had said, he had not even mentioned it. Ah, the smart one
smiled. He hitched again at the shoulders of his gown and said "Ah, I

doubt if one needs to remind a young woman about a knife when she is undergoing assault." The girl spoke out at that, she said "He told me he never went anywhere without his knife. He never knew when he could need it." The man's own lawyer tried to answer. That could mean anything, he said.

"It could mean he liked peeling fruit?" the prosecutor said. In that stagey way of his he simply held the knife up again and for once he said nothing. And somewhere through it all—because he could not remember the day exactly, that was half the trouble, Clem thought—a doctor said there was no doubt what had taken place. There was bruising on the girl's wrist, and contusion on the leg Clem had seen knock against the steps. The doctor confirmed that the marks on the man's face were clearly from the girl's nails. Yes, he agreed, they were the kind of wound a woman might well inflict who was defending herself.

Clem was dog-tired after the day in court. He had not looked forward to it and then it was worse than any expectation. He now kept coming back to the one thought, that somehow he had let down the man who had passed him, who had never noticed him. And yet for God's sake he couldn't do much more, Clem told himself, there were all those others as well, they believed them and not me. Yet it was two people fighting in distress or regret or in anger after sex, it wasn't what the court believed. He remembered the insolent sly movement of the girl's eyes as she saw and at once dismissed him at the top of the steps. And in court she was like a child almost, as she looked down when the doctor asked her questions, when she went back to sit beside her mother. While the man had looked like a liar or at least a fool when he took so long with his answers and refused to face directly at the court. His hands washed over each other while he was questioned, his shirt had been tucked up with the collar of his suit coat so that he looked untidy as well as dumb. He was like a man who wanted to say he was guilty, Clem thought, while the girl stood there well-dressed and confident, she was one of our own. Her mother had held her hand much of the time. And further back in the court among the Islanders there were two women in bright long dresses. One of them was elderly, her tight springy hair changing color, neither black nor reddish nor gray, so that it made Clem think it seemed singed. Beside her sat a much younger woman, perhaps her daughter. He watched that woman at the recesses during the day. When she stood with the group of dark men by the patch of lawn outside the courthouse there was such quietness about her. Then it came to him that she had the look of people who are balancing something, alert yet self-absorbed, while the older woman leaned against one of the men and cried. Her hair was smooth and drawn back with a lip at the side of her neck, then flowed out again across her shoulders. When she moved the light glanced off her hair and Clem wondered if she was the man's wife. He wanted to go and say to her, I've told the truth even if it's not enough, even if he made love to her it was only that, it wasn't more than that. The woman raised her eyes and looked at him and then looked past him.

That night before he slept Clem lay with the cat on his chest, his fingers moving in the soft fur. The animal's body vibrated with contentment. Clem was too tired to watch a program he usually liked, too shot for anything. But next morning he woke too early, and felt unwell. The unhappy time with Nan had kept returning to him in broken yet realistic dreams. There were those days again at her bedside when she would no longer speak to him, and the night not long before the end when she had turned, suddenly conscious and alert, watching him with her bright sunken eyes. She had said to him as she covered her thin speckled hand with his own, "It doesn't matter in the long run you know."

"Matter?" he had said.

"Whether we had those years or not." And there was a pause then, he had leaned forward so that his head was close against her own.

"Not mattered." She spoke lucidly and quietly, and he had sat there at her bedside appalled at what she said. A nurse who was in the room said to him, a few minutes later, when Nan's eyes were closed, "It's all confused with drugs. You mustn't think she knows." The nurse even touched his shoulder, she was trying to cover up for the dreadful clarity of death. He sat on with his fingers meeting around Nan's wrist. He knew that what the nurse had said to comfort him was wrong. He knew Nan had never spoken so surely to him in all their lives together. And what held him then was *that* was her final truth, the fact he must sit and watch until the machinery stopped. For that is what we are, he was thinking, we are machines for pain, for these last days of dissolution and denial, as though the sun had never shone on us, as though everything we ever took from music or family or God whatever it might be, must now be paid for with words like that, the indignity of denying what we always loved.

He had sat on with her until she stirred and asked for water, which he gave her from a teaspoon. She then lay back and watched the corner of the room, and then her lids again were lowered. He had sat until an hour later. the nurse again had touched his arm and led him from the room, because in his thinking of Nan he had not noticed when she left. Then like anything else, as he liked to say, Clem adapted to the silent house, a new routine. There was then a life of shopping and library books, watching TV and taking walks. Once a week he had a meal at his sister's, he visited a friend at the hospice off Shelly Beach Road, he fed and talked with his cat. Those things were mixed in his dreams too, the night after the court. Then he watched the sky lighten, and from the grayness of the first light he saw the day pick out the gilt frame of Nan's old-fashioned mirror, the bright towel at the end of his bed. He closed his eyes again and this time he slept comfortably. When he woke for a second time his mind was calm. He thought without distress about the people he must face again in a few hours' time, the girl whom he knew was lying and the Islander who was like a wild thing caught in a light too strong for it. It was so clear now that he thought of it. He would ask the Islander's lawyer to question him once more. If the lawyer drew him out, that was the thing, the way you saw them doing it all the time on TV. Then that young woman in the long colored dress, he would watch her face when it began to dawn on all of them in the courtroom that the man had told the truth, that it was Clem who made them believe it. If he could only watch that.

How odd it all is, Clem kept thinking as he moved about the kitchen, tidying up after his cup of tea and his piece of toast and his glass of Ribena. Odd how our moods can change even at my age, how much in these past couple of weeks I have passed through, feared, remembered, been ashamed of...He shaved and looked at himself in the bathroom mirror. He snipped at two loose hairs at the side of his neat moustache. The scissor's were Nan's, something she had kept from her girlhood, from the year before they had met. There was a paua shell inlay along the flattened grips for your fingers. Clem tilted the scissors for a moment and watched how the irridescent greens and blues ran against each other, merged into a kind of soft remote fire below the smooth surface of the shell. He snipped again at hair growing from his ears. You had to watch yourself all right, you could see it with some of those elderly ones he spoke to up at the library or swapped a few words with in the shops. Suddenly you noticed how they had let themselves go, there were stains on their cardigans or they weren't properly buttoned, and there were others even worse, the ones people moved away from. As long as you watched yourself, Clem thought, you were probably all right.

He was dressed and ready well ahead of time. He could stroll up the bus stop and even walk round Queen Street for a bit, before he took another bus up to the courthouse. That hill was past him now, although he liked it as much as anything in Auckland. The big palms in the park, the clumps of flax-like leaves with the orange flaring blooms like flying birds, and further up those trees with the huge gray roots lying along the ground—he would come back that way this afternoon. Along past the university and the floral clock that used to have begonias set out to make the numerals, he wondered if it still had them. God, it wasn't so long ago either to before the clock was even thought of, and he walked with Grandma along there. When he remembered that he could almost smell the warm fusty odor when the sun fell on her black skirt and he walked along beside her, his hand stretched up, clutching at her own. Don't snip your nails on my rings, love, she used to tell him. And at that corner where there used to be only grass he had stood looking up to a woman she spoke to, then at the great fat iron lady over there on her stand. She was as much the Queen of New Zealand as the Queen of England, didn't he know that? And the woman had given him a white lolly like a tiny satin cushion and asked him "There, won't you talk to me if I give you that?" And Grandma had puzzled him because he didn't have any money of his own and yet she said while she jiggled his arm

"You'll get no change out of this one."

Clem enjoyed the walk up to the bus. After yesterday's fleeting patches of sun, it was now clear and fine. From his gateway he looked down towards the water. The bridge and the yachts in the boat harbor were softened by a soft skein of mist. But up here one was above it. Mornings like this he used to lean on the rail of the ferry and watch the cliffs and the houses slide past. Days like this the colors seemed more vivid, even the brick sugar-works lifted up its yellow walls like—well, something more than you expected, somehow, and the sheet of water between the ferry and the approaching wharf was that deep green that slid off into blues, tilting and shimmering like those handles on the scissors.

Groups of girls from the convent passed him. They walked properly and there was no swinging their bags about and hollering to one another the way you'd see with some of those other kids up on the main road. He liked it that the older ones wore gloves when they walked past his house on Sundays. If he was on the veranda some of them would look up and say Good morning to him. Some of them made him think of horses, or of foals, rather, that long-legged grace a few of them had. He began to walk up the road and was caught up briefly in their current of youth and litheness, the sudden breaking of laughter from a group on the other side of the road. And then he knew there was a gray car slowly following him, drawing in towards the curb. It stopped when the policeman caught his eye. It was the same young chap who had come that morning several weeks ago and questioned him for the first time. Only then he had worn his cap down over his eyes, and now he sat with his blonde hair combed high, a kind of puff above his forehead. He beckoned Clem over as he opened the door and stepped out. Clem thought they must be giving him a ride to court for some reason. The policeman nodded up past the library to the main road. "Got you just in time, eh? Saved you a trip." He spoke while the old man watched his mouth so closely that he saw the way one of his bottom front teeth slightly tilted back, out of kilter with the rest, and there was the gray filling he could see in another tooth further back. The policeman said again, "Saved you the trip in." He touched the sides of his tie, carefully. "Our rapist did himself in."

When Clem said nothing the young man explained it again. "Cut his wrists," he said. He moved the side of one hand against his other wrist. "Had this razorblade tucked somewhere and that was that."

"Last night?" Clem heard himself ask.

"Last night, early this morning. There wasn't a chance when they found him anyway." Then the policeman gave this kind of laugh, his breath caught in as though he were going to cough. "Shows he must have done it all right. It's one way out of facing it." And now Clem was looking at the shining metal number on the uniformed shoulder and the slight golden growth of beard along the man's jaw-line. The man must be finishing work, Clem thought, he can't just be starting or he'd have shaved. Then the policeman rested his hand for a moment on Clem's shoulder. "Don't you think about it any more, Pop. Nothing we could have done." He stooped back into the car and placed his cap back on his head. He glanced up for a second into the rear vision mirror and made sure the cap sat on straight. "Right," he said to the driver. As the car edged from the side of the footpath he spoke again, leaning from the lowered window. "Not to worry now, OK Pop?"

"No," Clem was saying. "I won't." He had no idea why he said it, or why he repeated it when the car had gone. A woman going towards the shops saw him speaking to himself and looked away from him. He continued to walk up the road, up the little distance to the Post Office and the green slatted seats near the taxi rank. The first time he knew Nan was crook was when she had said "I'll have to sit here for a minute, Clem." It was pension day and they had just left the Post Office. And now Clem sat there again and looked past the brown iron railings at the top of the men's public lavatory and across to the corner opposite, to the Islanders near that travel shop that advertised Pacific flights. One of the men wore a deep collar of flowers round his neck. There was a woman with them too, he could see her mouth open from here while she laughed and for a second rested her arm against the shoulder of one of the men. *Cut his wrists* the policeman had said. He had moved his pale hand like that, like a saw, against his own wrist. The blood and snot and tears on the man's face running up the steps and passing him under the light at the end of the street, and now this, that movement at his wrists—it's

115

as if there was no time between that pain and then this, Clem thought, that man breathless and crying because of the girl, waiting in his cell, taking the blade from where it was hidden. And he must have been thinking of her when he did that too, and of the woman with the face that looked like it was carved, the one stepping onto the grass outside the court, turning from the men, the bright patterned skirt pulling tight against her body. *His wrists* and that would mean waiting too, Clem had read once how many minutes. And in the dark he supposed he would only feel his bleeding, it would have no color. Does a man keep his eyes say on a light outside a window, on a corner of a room, until these things ebb, until they waver maybe, waver as though dipped in water? Or lie with his eyes closed so that the last thing is not the ordinary things, the table, the chairs, but the last thing you decide on to fill your mind, the last gift to oneself? Can one bring that off, Clem thought. And he said aloud as though he was at home and not where people moved close to him, up and down the steps of the Post Office, "I want to know that. I've got to know it."

Born in 1937, Vincent O'Sullivan has published six volumes of poetry, two collections of short stories, and edited both prose and verse anthologies. "The Witness Man" won the 1979 Katherine Mansfield Short Story Award. Mr. O'Sullivan is currently editing the 4 volumes of Katherine Mansfield's Letters.

"He stood there for a while, taking in
the huddle of houses, the people talking in a
language he could not understand,
absorbing the feel of exotic distances."

Tong

BY F. SIONIL JOSÉ

CONRADO Lopez fell deeply in love for the first time when he was thirty. It was one of those beautiful things destined to bleakness and from the very beginning, he had an inkling that this was how it would be. And all because Alice Tan was Chinese.

When he first saw her, it seemed as if she had blossomed straight out of a Chinese art book; she had a complexion as clear as it was fair. When he got to know her better, he used to trace the blue veins in her arms, the blood vessels in her cheeks. Her nose was perfect, and her Chinese eyes had a brightness that could dispel the gloom which came over him. Long afterwards, when he remembered her eyes, how she looked, how she smiled, an intense feeling akin to physical pain would lance him.

Alice Tan's parents used to run a small grocery store in Ongpin; both came from Fookien and Alice could trace her family back to Amoy. Conrado Lopez did not know his lineage beyond his great grandfather and was not interested in the Chinese traditional kinship system. But he got so interested afterwards, he started to delve into his own background. He lived with his spinster sister, Remedios, in a small house in Makata, a side street parallel to Rizal Avenue in Santa Cruz. He had inherited the house with its pocket-size yard from his parents. The lower floor, which had its own entrance, was rented out to a lawyer who was adept at fixing things at City Hall. He and his sister lived on the second floor which had two bedrooms, a living-dining room and a toilet and kitchen with antique fixtures. His sister looked after the house, his clothes and his general well-being. Conrado had finished accounting at one of the Azacarraga universities and would have amounted to something more than just being an accountant in Makati but he had let opportunities pass—opportunities which would have taken him away from Manila and his older sister whom he supported. It was because of such responsibility that he had never really been serious with any girl.

He was unprepared for Alice Tan; in fact, in the beginning, he was not sure at all about his feelings for her. It started in March when brownouts were frequent so that when the lights went out that early evening, he thought it was another brownout. But he noticed that the lights in the other houses were on so he immediately concluded there must be something wrong with the fuse. He always kept an extra fuse so he threw the main switch off and changed it. But he had hardly thrown the switch on when the line in the ceiling started sputtering. Then a loud report and darkness.

By now, Meding was alarmed but Conrado assured her the house would not burn down as long as the switches were off. He dashed off to Bambang two blocks away to one of the electrical shops there.

He had passed the New Life Electrical Supply a few times but had rarely looked in; for one, he never bought electrical supplies in the neighborhood as he always bought them in the supermarket in Makati. It was then that he saw Alice Tan; she was in jeans and a *katsa* blouse with a high, lace collar and long sleeves that imparted to her an appearance at once regal and demure.

It was not a big shop. It carried hardware, nails, ropes, flashlights, but mostly electrical goods. She sat behind the glass counter and when he came in, she put down the weekly women's magazine she was reading.

"I don't think I will need an electrician," he said. "It is just a burned line, I think. I put the switch off."

"That is the first thing one should do," she said with a professional tone. "I think you will need rubberized tape, and a pair of new fuses."

"I am sure of that," he said. "But how do I go about fixing it?" He was not too sure now, having forgotten most of his physics classes in high school; the positive, the negative...

"Simple," she said, bringing out a roll of blue tape from the counter. "The lines should never get mixed up. When the covering is worn out and they cross each other, that's when the trouble starts."

"It is like a boy and a girl then," he said with a laugh. "If they really get mixed up, there's bound to be some result..."

She smiled at his little joke. "I hope you are not fooling me," she said.

"You can come to my house—it's close by, in Makata," he said. "It is dark."

"I believe you," she said. "Well then, first see to it that the main switch is off. Then look for the line that was burned. Sometimes rats gnaw the line. If you touch it and it is live..."

"I will not forget that," he said.

"Clean the wires, then tape them individually. See to it that they do not meet. That they do not touch."

"No touch, no fireworks," he said. "Thanks for the lesson."

In three months, Conrado Lopez learned a bit more about electricity and a lot about Alice Tan. She was studying in one of the Recto universities in the mornings and in the afternoons, immediately after school, she came to the shop where she had lunch, usually cooked by her aunt. At eight in the evening, she walked to Avenida for her ride to Ongpin and the apartment she shared with her brothers. She seldom went out even on the Sundays when the shop was closed. She looked at television or played ping-pong in one of the Chinese clubs in Binondo.

Conrado Lopez took to having a late *merienda* at the shabby Chinese restaurant across the street. The restaurant was never full—there was always an empty table dirty with noodle droppings and dried blobs of beer, the loud talk of jeepney drivers who frequented the place, and the juke box oozing Rico Puno and Nora Aunor songs. It was a good place to watch Alice Tan as she went about her chores.

Many a night, too, he would return to the restaurant for a cup of bad coffee and wait for her to leave and walk the short stretch to her jeepney stop, sometimes with him just a few steps behind.

In three months, too, Conrado could have opened a small shop for electrical supplies. He was buying yet another light bulb when Alice finally accosted him.

"I will not sell it to you," she said simply.

He was taken aback.

"I don't know what you are trying to do but I know you are not buying the goods to use. You don't need all those bulbs. I have been counting them. A light bulb lasts more than six months. You have bought more than a dozen in a month."

"I like changing them, you know, different watts."

"Mr. Lopez, tell me the truth."

"I also like collecting lengths of electric wire, sockets, rubber tapes. Have you heard of Thomas Alva Edison? Maybe, I am an inventor..."

"You are a liar," Alice Tan said, her eyes crinkling in a smile.

Conrado Lopez melted. "Yes, a terrible liar, am I not?"

"What really are you trying to do?"

Conrado Lopez stammered. "I...I wanted to talk with you. I want to see you. I enjoy talking with you. That's the simple truth. Believe me. And I don't mind buying all this useless stuff as long as I can see you..."

"But you can talk with me anytime as long as there are no customers. My uncle does not mind..."

He sighed. "That is good to know. But I was not sure. You are Chinese..."

"I am a human being," she said. "Will you stop buying things then?"

"No, I cannot come here without a reason. I must talk with you again even if I have to spend doing it..."

She appeared thoughtful. "All right, as long as it is not too often. And there are no customers..."

The door at the rear opened and Alice's uncle came in with a cup of coffee. He looked at Conrado without a flicker of recognition then sat before his table, impassive and still.

"Thank you, Miss Tan," Conrado said gratefully.

The following night, he finally found the courage to walk up to her. She thought, perhaps, he was one of those bag snatchers who had become so blatantly open. Her first impulse was to hold her bag tightly and draw away when he moved closer to greet her.

"You frightened me, Mr. Lopez," she said.

Bambang was never brightly lit. They walked slowly. "I would like to take you home," he said. "But I don't have a car. We can take a taxi if you like."

"I prefer *calesas*," she said, "but it is such a fine evening, can we walk?"

Indeed, an evening washed with rain, the street glistening. Home was quite a distance but it pleased him nonetheless for they would have a lot of time to talk.

He asked how long she had lived in Ongpin and she said, all her life, that she was familiar with its alleys, its shops, just as he knew Makata and Bambang and Misericordia—these were the names of the streets of his boyhood as he remembered them.

"We are Ongpin Chinese," she said. "Do you know what that means?"

He shook his head.

"That means we are not rich," she said. "The rich Chinese are in Greenhills. That's where they live anyway. Before the war, they said it was in Santa Mesa."

He did not realize there were social distinctions among the Chinese, too; he had always thought they were all of the same class, that they were all Fookienese, and that to a man, they looked down on the Filipinos, what with their Chinese *tong* associations, their schools.

He wondered if this was the time to bring out his cliche sentiments and he worried that if he did, he would be creating a barrier between them. He decided it was better to be frank, to be honest.

His difficulty was that he could not quite trust his feelings no matter how strong they were; he did not know enough about the

Chinese really. "I must just as well admit, Alice," he said, "that I have some views on our Chinese problem. I am really glad that the Chinese schools have been taken over by the Department of Education, that we have relations with Peking now. But if I had my way, all those Chinese schools should have been closed a long time ago..."

"What don't you like in us?" she asked, looking at him briefly, a smile darting across her face, a smile so pretty that it disarmed him completely.

"Your clannishness, for one," he said.

"But you are clannish, too," she said. "Look at all the people in power; they are either Ilokanos or from Leyte."

"Chinese girls never marry Filipino boys. It is always the other way around."

"You call us *Intsik Baboy.*"

"Because it is true—you are filthy. No, not you personally."

"And the Filipinos are stupid. Not you personally," she mimicked him.

He checked himself. "Hey," he said, "on our first time together—and look, we are quarreling."

"You started it," she said petulantly.

"I don't like quarrels. Can you imagine how it would be if we were married?"

"You are going too fast," she said. "Now, you are talking about us being married. We barely know each other."

"After all those things I bought from you? I could start another store..."

"I don't want your money wasted," she said. "Give them back to me and I will sell them for you."

They had reached Recto and had crossed over, the air around them now thick with the scent of rotting vegetables and chicken droppings as they passed the public market. They walked on through a dimly lit neighborhood, the street pocked with craters, the gutter slimy with refuse and mud. Beyond, the lights of Ongpin shone, Chinese characters in red and blue. Now, the sidewalk was red brick, the shops bright with red candles, gold leaf pictures. *Calesas* jostled each other on the street and the uneven sidewalk was crammed with fruit stalls. Around them, the smell of Chinese cooking, of incense and acrid oils, the wail of Chinese flutes. They went beyond a stone arch, bright green and red, and a creek which befouled the air, then turned right and after a few steps, she stopped. "This is as far as you go. I live over there," she said, pointing to an alley.

"But I want to see you to your door. I am not hiding. I am a bachelor. My intentions are honorable. I would like to visit your house, maybe not tonight, but someday, meet your parents..."

"I have no parents," she said. "I have three brothers and I am the youngest. My uncle—Mr. Tan, you have seen him in the store, he is our guardian; he took care of us when we were young..."

"I still would like to see where you live," he said.

"No," she was firm and there was an edge to her voice. "This is as far as you go, or you will not walk me home again."

He did not argue. "Is it because I am Filipino?" he asked dully, as she turned to go. She took three, four steps, then she turned, and shook her head.

He watched till she entered the alley and disappeared in its black maw. He stood there for a while, taking in the huddle of houses, the people talking in a language he could not understand, absorbing the feel of exotic distances. Then it started to drizzle.

The following evening, Conrado Lopez passed by the shop before proceeding to the Chinese restaurant across the street. Her uncle was not there but Alice was and as he passed, their eyes locked. He positioned himself in the restaurant, toying with his cup of coffee, and watched her reading a magazine. Soon it was time to close. Mr. Tan went out to pull the steel accordion door shut, and it was then that Conrado noticed the black Mercedes in front of the shop to which, as if she was in a hurry, Alice went. She sat in front with the driver and as they drove off, in the soft dark, he could see her turn and take a last look at him.

He now realized with some apprehension, of panic even, that she was being cordoned off, and he wondered if this was her doing, if she did not really want to talk with him again. He reproached himself for having talked so openly when what he should have done was to say the usual niceties. In his office that Saturday, he asked to be excused in the afternoon. He proceeded to Bambang at once; he must see her, apologize to her, anything to have her talk with him again, walk with him again.

She was at the store and he was vastly relieved when he saw that her uncle was not at his table. The moment Conrado went in, however, her eyes told him that this was not the time to talk. "I am sorry," he said, barely raising his voice above a whisper, "but I would like to see you again."

He could not continue for the door at the rear opened and Mr. Tan came in, a coil of electric wiring in his arms.

Without his telling her, Alice stood up, got a bulb from the shelf and tested it. "It is three pesos and eighty centavos," she said, wrapping it in a sheet of old newspaper. She took some time writing the receipt while Mr. Tan brought down another roll of wiring from the rack and started measuring a length.

"It is in the receipt," she told Conrado, handing him the receipt. "The receipt," she repeated with a smile.

That evening, as he and his sister sat down to dinner, he told her about Alice Tan. "I have been thinking about our life," he said. "I don't think we would need to spend much more if I got married..."

Meding looked at him; she was fifteen years older but she had taken good care of herself and really looked no older than forty or so. She could have easily got married—there was still that chance if she had a mind to—but she had been reclusive. It had often bothered Conrado to think that she had not got married so that she "could take care of him."

"And if I do get married, you will continue to live with us, of course, like it always has been. How does the idea look to you, *Ate?*"

He had expected her to sulk and was pleasantly surprised when she beamed. "I have often wondered when it would be," she said. "I am sure by now you know the right kind of girl..."

It was then that he told her she was Chinese, that he was interested in having them meet...He did not realize till then the depths of his ignorance about his sister's feelings, but from the expression on her face, he knew at once that Alice Tan—if and when the moment came—would have difficulty living in the same house with her.

Through the night, he could not sleep, wondering how he would be able to talk with her, to see her without that black Mercedes tailing them, without Mr. Tan eavesdropping on them. Sunday morning, he decided to go to Ongpin, to the maze of wooden houses and shops that made up Chinatown. He went up the alley where she had disappeared in the night; it was a dead end, a dark and dispirited place, flanked by decrepit apartment houses, with laundry in the windows and a pile of garbage at the end. Children were playing in the alley, and the houses were filled with people who did not once look at him as he passed. He peered briefly into open doorways, and soon reached the dead end without seeing her. He walked back to the main street clogged with *calesas* and vehicles and entered the first movie house he passed. It was a Kung Fu movie in Chinese, without subtitles and he could not understand a word but with all that action, dialogue was hardly necessary. It was when he finally came out, long past noon, that he remembered how Alice gave him his receipt. She had repeated, "the receipt." Then, it struck him, what she was trying to say. He grabbed a taxi and hoped to God that his sister had not emptied the wastebasket where he had thrown the piece of paper. Breathless, he dashed to his room and was greatly relieved to find the receipt still there. Sure enough, in her legible penmanship: "Rizal Park Post Office, Sunday four p.m."

He looked at his watch; it was three fifty. By no miracle could he get there in ten minutes but just the same, he raced down to Avenida and told the taxi driver to hurry, in heaven's name. It had started to rain when they crossed the Pasig and it was really pouring when he reached the Park Post Office in front of the Manila Hotel. He was also fifteen minutes late. He dashed from the cab to the shade of the Post Office marquee. He cursed himself not so much for not bringing an umbrella but for being so stupid as not to have understood what Alice wanted him to know. She must have got tired waiting and had left. He sat, wet and forlorn, on the stone ledge. Maybe, if he went to her apartment—that was what his sister always said, that a man whose intentions are honorable should always visit the girl in her house.

The rain whipped the Park in gusty sheets. It was stormy weather and beyond the Park, the Walled City and all of Manila seemed enveloped with mist. But in half an hour, the rain diminished, then stopped altogether and in the direction of the Bay, the dark clouds were rimmed with silver.

It was Alice Tan who was late and it was good that he did not leave; he saw her get out of her taxi and his heart leaped and pounded so hard he could hear it. He ran to her and hardly heard her apologies, how she had difficulty leaving; he was aware of nothing else but this creature who had come bringing light to this dismal afternoon.

They walked to the sea and now, with the rain that still threatened the city, they had the whole sea wall to themselves.

"I am stupid," he said, "for not having understood when you said, it is in the receipt."

"I was worried about that," she said, sitting close to him so that their arms touched. "Filipinos are like that, anyway. *Gong.*"

"What's that?"

"Stupid, like you said."

"Now," he said. "I hope we will not start an argument again. What don't you like in us, anyway?"

"First," she said, "you are lazy. You don't know what industry is— and this is why, no matter what your leaders say, you will never amount to anything."

"You don't know what you are saying. We work very hard," he said. "Our farmers work very hard."

"My father used to wake up at four in the morning," Alice Tan said with pride. "And we never went to sleep earlier than eleven o'clock at night."

"Many Filipinos are like that."

"Show me," she said. "And then, you are so corrupt. Why, almost every week, someone goes to the shop—policemen, revenue agents, all of them. All they want is money. My uncle always gives, of course. And everytime, he increases the price of what we sell. In the end, it is the customer who suffers."

"He is just as guilty then," Conrado told her.

"My father had to pay a bribe of ten thousand pesos—way back in 1950—for his citizenship. It almost broke him.

"So you are a Filipino citizen then," he said. "This is where you make your living, where the rich Chinese and your uncle make their money, exploiting the country, its resources, its people. If you don't like it here—why don't you go back to Peking or Taipei, whichever you choose?"

"Be careful now," she told him. "You misunderstand me completely. My oldest brother—he was very impressed with what the communists were doing in Peking. He went there and returned, disillusioned. It was not so much that the life there is harsh...it was that he did not feel at home. Can you not see, Conrado? Our home is here. China—it would be foreign to me, although I could get sentimental about it. I just want this country to have better things—less corruption, less enmity, less poverty..."

He realized then that he had spoken again in a way that wouldn't endear him to her. He was determined to salvage the afternoon. "It is just as well that we have our arguments now. For when we get married..."

The waves lapped on the rocks below them. She turned to him, wonder in her eyes. "Please don't talk about something impossible," she said. "Let us just be friends..."

"But I am serious," he said. "I am not making a lot. Just a thousand and a half a month. Plus that four hundred pesos rent from the house. I can support you, not in style. But I have a career still ahead of me. You can go on with your schooling if you want to. We may have some problems with my sister but she will adjust. Why don't we go and meet her? There's just the two of us..."

It was then that she told him. "It cannot be, Conrado. I have been promised in marriage to someone already. There is just a little time for us..."

For the rest of his life, Conrado Lopez would never really know why Alice Tan saw him again, and still again, every Sunday at four p.m. in the park. When he took her back to Ongpin that evening, she had extracted from him a promise that he should never go to the shop again, or sit like some corner thug in that restaurant across the street where it was obvious to her uncle even that he was watching her. He got her address in Ongpin and he promised, too, that he would never go there unless it was for some very, very serious reason. She would see him again that Sunday and the Sundays thereafter. Now, at least, Conrado Lopez had something to look forward to. He went eagerly back to his history books, to the references on the Chinese, Limahong, the Parian, the galleon trade which carried Chinese silks and other luxury goods to Mexico thence to Europe. He asked the Chinese embassy in Roxas for handouts and in the bookshops in Avenida, he searched for pocketbooks and other bargains that described China. He even fancied himself learning Mandarin and going to a Buddhist temple although Alice Tan had told him that she was Protestant.

On the next Sunday, the sun was out; a storm had just blown over and the grass was soggy. Alice Tan arrived in a blue print dress; it was the first time he saw her in a dress and her legs, as he had always suspected, were shapely. They went to the Manila Hotel for a cup of coffee—that was all that he could afford when he studied the menu and he warned her about it. This time, they did not argue. Instead, she told him about herself, that it was her dream—as it was the dream of most Chinese girls—to get married and raise a family. She had gone out with Chinese boys to discos in Makati and had exchanged confidences with her Chinese girl friends who had dated Filipino boys and they were all agreed that their Filipino dates were more interesting, for their Chinese dates talked of nothing but business. And yes, she said with a slight laugh, they told her, too, that Filipino boys were quicker and that they made better lovers.

"And now," he said, "you would like to find out for yourself."

She unwrapped the special *hopia* that she had brought while an amused waitress looked on. A couple of Chinese boys passed; they stared at her so she whispered to him: "See? They never like Chinese girls to date Filipino boys. They think Filipino boys are just making fools of us..."

"Am I?" he asked.

She reached across the table and almost spilled the goblet, held his hand and pressed it.

On the fifth Sunday, Conrado Lopez took Alice Tan to one of the motels on M.H. del Pilar. The August sky was threatened with rain clouds, it had become dark and they had embraced behind the palms near the sea wall. He had told her simply that he wanted to hold her, make love to her and she had not replied but had, instead, kissed him with passion. They walked to the boulevard and hailed a taxi. She sat wordless beside him, and even when they had finally entered the motel garage, and the door had shut behind them, still, she did not speak.

Only when they were finally in the room, her face flushed, his hands eager and his whole being aflame, did she tell that she had expected this to happen, but not too soon.

She was a virgin and the sheet was soiled. They lay together for a long time and he told her what he knew of the old days, how the Filipino groom would hang the blood-stained blanket by the window the following morning for all his relatives to see. And she said it was the same in Old China.

It was when they made ready to leave that she started to cry, the sobs torn out of her in pain and trembling. He embraced her, kissed her cheeks wet with tears, her hair.

"We will get married in the morning—if this is what worries you," he said. "Now—if you wish, we can walk to the Malate Church and ask. I did not do this to take advantage of you, to fool you..."

"I know," she said, pressing closer still to him.

"Then what are you crying about?"

"I cannot marry you," she said.

He drew her away and looked at her tear-stained face.

"Is it because you are Chinese?"

She nodded.

"But you love me, you said so. I am not rich but you will not starve..."

"It is not the money."

"If it is not the money...?"

"Tradition, custom. Whatever you call it."

"Hell with it!" Conrado cursed in his breath.

Then it came out. "My uncle, Conrado. He took care of us when we were orphaned. I told you. And there is this rich Chinese who lives in Greenhills. He is a widower. He has helped my uncle. Given my brothers very good jobs..."

He drew farther from her, looked at her, beautiful and true and then he went to her, hugged her. "Don't, Alice," he said in a voice hoarse with entreaty. "Let us elope. Let us go to my house now. They cannot find you there..."

She looked at him and shook her head. "I am Chinese," she said simply.

When he passed the shop that Monday, he was surprised to see she was not at the counter; he hurried around the block, and when he got to the shop again, she was still not there. He returned shortly before eight when Mr. Tan would bring the accordion iron shutter down but neither the black Mercedes nor Alice were there. Every day that week, he passed by the shop. Sunday, he went to the Park and stayed there till dark.

That Monday afternoon, straight from his office, he went to see Mr. Tan. There was no hint of recognition in the face of Alice's uncle— just this bland, expressionless mien, as Conrado introduced himself.

"Where is Alice, Mr. Tan?" he finally asked.

He replied in excellent Tagalog; Alice was no longer working in the shop.

"Where can I find her then?"

The Chinese shook his head and did not reply.

"Mr. Tan," he said in a voice which quavered. "I know you don't like a Filipino husband for your niece. But I love her and I want to marry her. You think I am interested in her money—then don't give her any dowry. No dowry, is that clear?" He took his wallet out and drew a calling card, laid it on the counter. "I have a good job with a big firm. I am young and industrious. I can support her and I can even continue sending her to school. I know you took care of her and I am grateful."

The Chinese shook his head again and this time, he smiled, gold teeth flashing, and held Conrado Lopez' arm across the counter. "Don't misunderstand," he said. "But you are very, very late. You must leave and don't bother us anymore. There is nothing I can do for you..."

"What don't you like in me?" he asked tersely as he backed away into the noisy sidewalk.

He had memorized the address which she had given him. He took a taxi to Ongpin. It was very dark, the neon lights were on. He walked up the alley, and when he got to the door, 14-D, on it was posted a sign in Chinese. A young man was at the next door playing a guitar and he asked where the people next door were. "They have moved," he said, "to Greenhills." Did he know the street? The number? No. And what is this sign? "For rent," the young man said.

For many days, it was as if Conrado Lopez was in a daze, in a limbo without rim. After office hours, he would wander around the shops in Binondo in the hope that he would see her visiting the old neighborhood. He made a list of the best Chinese restaurants in the city and on occasion, visited them specially at night when there were parties attended by the wealthy Chinese. He would wait in their lobbies, watching, searching.

On Sundays and holidays, he frequented the supermarket in Greenhills knowing this was where the wealthy Chinese shopped and many a time, he would hurry after what seemed a familiar back, a turn of the head, only to find it was not her.

He took to compulsively reading on China until he was quite familiar with contemporary happenings there. On Sundays, he made a round of Ongpin and even got to visiting funeral parlors—"La Paz" particularly, where the Chinese held the wake for their dead. And twice, he went to Benavides, to the air-conditioned Protestant chapel there, hoping that Alice would attend a service.

He no longer went to the Park except one Sunday in mid-February; it was a cool, pleasant afternoon with a pure blue sky. He sat on the stone ledge as he had done in the past. It was four and for a time, he was lost in reverie, remembering how it was the first time, the splashing rain, the anxiety that he would miss her.

It was then that he noticed the black Mercedes parked at the edge of the green and beyond it, Alice walking to the car, her arm held by a fat, bald Chinese, old enough to be her father. She was big with child and as she looked at Conrado, there was this brief, anguished look on her face which told him not to move, not to speak. She got into the car, her husband after her, and as they drove away, he still stood there reeling with emotion, knowing clearly now what it was all about, the *tong* that must be paid, the life that must be warped because it had to be lived.

Born in 1924, F. Sionil José was encouraged to enjoy literature and to write by two teachers, one in grade school and the other at the University of Santo Tomas. He founded the Philippine Center of International PEN in 1958. In 1980 he received the Ramon Magsaysay Award for journalism, literature and creative communication arts.

"He was a master of his craft,
and as light-fingered as a butterfly."

The Big Deal

BY ROSALIND MORTON

THE bench at the side of the parking lot was a good vantage point.
Piet often sat there. He found it paid dividends. It was a convenient
place for shoppers to leave their cars. Consequently, it gave him
plenty of scope.

He opened his newspaper at random. He always carried a
newspaper, usually picked up on a park bench, or out of a dustbin. It
was seldom the latest edition, but Piet cared little about what was in
the newspaper, unless it happened to be fish and chips. He used it as
a screen, and he wasn't always careful enough to have it the right
way up.

His slight figure in his dirty, shabby clothes rarely attracted
attention. Peeping cautiously around, he could watch the world go
by and spot the unwary. He was a master of his craft, and as light-
fingered as a butterfly. He could slip a wallet out of a hip pocket, flick
it into his folded newspaper and continue his innocent-looking stroll

down the street, without giving away his action either to the victim or the passerby.

Oh yes, he made a nice living. He had quite a little hoard stacked away in his dingy room. He wouldn't trust a bank with his money, not he. They might want to know where he had got it.

He had also had some useful little hauls from parked cars. He scented, like a ferret, the careless driver who didn't bother to lock his car, and he usually managed to find something worth taking. If it turned out to be of no use to him, Joe at the pawnship would nearly always give him something for it, and he didn't ask awkward questions.

Today things seemed rather quiet. He felt hungry and decided to buy a pie. He was just folding his newspaper, preparatory to taking a stroll to get the pie and seek better prospects, when he saw a young couple approaching. The man was carrying a heavy box. They came to the car parked right beside him. What a piece of luck that was. Piet quickly retired behind his newspaper and feigned sleep.

Peering through half-closed eyes, he noticed that the box was done up very securely. The couple had a somewhat urgent, almost furtive look about them, and the girl looked flush and nervous.

"Bill, I don't like leaving it in the car. Will it be all right?"

"Of course, silly, I'll lock the car and we won't be long. But come what may, I must have some coffee and a bite to eat before we get going. Then we'll make a dash for it and drive like blazes, and we should be in Port Elizabeth just after dark."

"Is the car all right? I mean, we don't want to have a break down on the way, not with that lot on board, do we?"

"We won't have any trouble, I promise you. I've had the car checked and it's 100%," Bill said.

"Oh I wish we'd never got into this racket. I'm scared I tell you. And what are we going to do when we get there?"

"Judy, my love, stop worrying. I've contacted them and there'll be one of them waiting for us. Nothing will go wrong; I've made certain of that. I know where the place is. All we have to do is hand over the box, and our worries will be over."

"Boy, will I be glad," said Judy fervently. "Quite frankly, I'm not enjoying this one bit, and I hope you never do it again."

"Oh relax honey, you worry too much."

The couple gave no indication of having noticed Piet—he did have the protection of a tree trunk, which screened him from view. Also, he had the ability of making himself appear small and inconspicuous.

He listened eagerly to their conversation while they put the box carefully into the car and locked it securely.

"There we are," said Bill. "Everything is locked, and now for some food. I'm starving."

Excitement welled up in Piet. He wanted to dash to the car, unlock the door and get at this precious parcel. This, he felt sure, was going to be a really memorable haul—something big.

He lowered his newspaper and watched impatiently as they waited for the traffic to allow them to cross the road to a tearoom on the other side of the street. Elated as he was at the promising prospect, he restrained himself, and his movements were casual and unobtrusive, despite the fact that there were few people about to notice him.

He peered into the car, and there it was. It was the most promising parcel he had ever had the good fortune to pick up. It was so beautifully and carefully wrapped, it could only be something very special.

" 'Struth, this is my lucky day," he said softly to himself. "I can't wait to open it. I reckon I'll make a packet this time."

Opening the car door was a simple matter to an expert like himself. The box was somewhat larger than he would have liked, and also fairly heavy. He hastily and deftly wrapped it in his newspaper. Removing his jacket, he draped it over the parcel and, wiping the car to remove fingerprints, he set off at a smart pace, though at the same time doing nothing to arouse suspicion.

Piet rented a shabby room in a slum area conveniently near to the parking lot. A few other people rented rooms in the same gloomy building. He knew none of them. It didn't suit him to get friendly with his neighbors. He preferred to ply his trade, if one could call it that, on his own. One never knew when people would talk, and then where would he be? In the jug, no doubt.

No, it was better to keep to one's self, especially when one was such a past master at the art. A clumsy amateur could ruin a brilliant maneuvre.

Some of the tenants tried to get into conversation with him when they met on the landing or the stairs. The garrulous old charwoman worried him persistently to clean his room, but he would have none of it. He wasn't going to have anyone poking around his belongings and finding out things he would prefer them not to know. She always had a bulging carrier bag with her, filled, he felt sure with pickings from the rooms of other tenants which she cleaned.

His line of "business" made him highly suspicious of other people. He knew all the tricks of the trade and could see through any subterfuge on the part of another. In short, he trusted nobody. Her eagerness to clean his room was obviously just a ruse to see what she could find to add to the contents of her carrier bag.

When he reached the rickety, dark staircase, he hurried up to his room. He put down the box carefully while he fumbled in his pockets for his key. When he finally found it, he let himself in and locked the door behind him. He put the box down on the floor in the sparsely furnished room, and on his knees began feverishly to open it. It wasn't an easy matter. The box was securely wired with many strands. There were, however, several tiny slits between the planks.

Breathing heavily in his greedy eagerness to lay hands on his haul, he rummaged in several boxes scattered about the floor of his untidy room until he found a pair of pliers, and wrenched first at one strand of wire and then another, gritting his teeth in the effort. But having removed the wire, he found that the lid was securely nailed down. He cursed softly.

Another feverish search in the boxes produced a claw hammer, and he prized the lid off with a certain amount of difficulty, but at last it was free.

He flung the lid back triumphantly—and after a second's stunned disbelief, he bounded in one mighty leap onto the dilapidated table and thence to the top of a small wardrobe, which teetered dangerously, emitting as he did so, sounds of the utmost terror.

Shivering and gibbering with fear on his rickety perch, he gazed mesmerized at the writhing bodies of six large cobras, the sweat glistening on his blanched face.

Glad to be out of the confinement of the box, the snakes explored their new surroundings with flickering tongues, gliding, curling, and twisting and turning, and now and then rearing up and raising their hoods.

This was, without a doubt, the most terrible moment of his life. Snakes had always filled him with unspeakable horror and revulsion. Now he felt that he would certainly die. One moment he wished he could die; the next, he was as much afraid of dying as he was of the snakes. What had he done to deserve such a fate as this. He thought he would go mad. He had never done anyone any harm—well, not what he called harm—certainly nothing as terrible as this.

At this time of day there was never anybody in the building, so shouting for help would be of little use, at any rate not until late in the evening. In any case, he had so often given the occupants a curt brush-off, that there was scant hope of any of them coming to his aid. Perhaps he could attract their attention if he called for long enough. He would just have to wait until he heard footsteps.

Now he understood why the girl had been afraid, and an unwilling partner in the undertaking. How well he understood. What kind of a man was that fellow who made up parcels of dangerous snakes. He would like to report him to the police. No, he could hardly do that. How would he explain how the parcel came to be in his possession? And in any case he had no wish to have anything to do with the police, no matter whose side they were on. But a man like this should not be allowed to be at large. He was a public danger.

Suddenly it occurred to him that it was all very well thinking up what he was going to do to this man. But what was to become of him? Would he die of starvation up here on top of the wardrobe, with a writhing snake pit beneath him, and nobody to help him. He was filled with misery and despair.

Perhaps he had been wrong to keep so much to himself. Suppose nobody came to help him, and for that matter, how could they help him. If they broke the lock on the door and came in and saw the snakes, they'd be off like greased lightning. If nobody answered his cries for help and he died on top of the wardrobe, would anyone notice that he was missing? He felt terribly alone. He wondered whether the old char would notice his absence. Perhaps it was a good thing that she was such a busybody. It was a ray of hope.

He had been so happy at picking up such a splendid parcel, and now all his dreams had been shattered. He had thought that this was going to be a really big deal. He felt the loss bitterly. He had been cheated. Had this been anyone else's loss and his gain, it would have caused him no qualms whatever. He would merely have said, "Well business is business."

"It's not right to put snakes in parcels," he muttered to himself, "and what for, I'd like to know."

Then, for the first time Piet noticed some writing on the lid of the box. It was addressed to:

> The Curator
> Snake Park
> Port Elizabeth

Rosalind Morton grew up on a farm in South Western Cape Province, a land of rivers, lakes and virgin forests. She is an outdoor person with a passion for mountaineering. She started writing at an early age and has numerous articles, short stories and plays to her credit.

"They wouldn't even allow a bird to fly over the treasury site."

The Rusty Tin Can in the Treasury

BY AZIZ NESIN

ONCE, twice, thrice upon a time, long long ago, there was a country on this earth with nothing. This country with nothing had a sultan and the sultan had a treasury. The nation's most valuable legacy was preserved in the treasury. The nation boasted about this legacy which was left them by their forefathers. They consoled themselves: "Even though we have nothing, at least this legacy was left us by our forefathers," and thus they tried to forget their poverty and destitution.

As the legacy from their forefathers belonged not to one or two persons but to the entire nation, everyone took a share in the bragging over this precious relic. They all endeavored with heart and soul to protect it.

In order to protect this relic, which belonged to the entire nation, the sultan's treasury being the most suitable place, it remained hidden there. Armed sentries guarded the treasury without blinking an eye. They wouldn't even allow a bird to fly over the treasury site.

The sultan, grand vizier, viziers, and all the notables of the palace, swore on their honor, one day every year, to protect this holy relic left by their ancestors.

Time came and went. Then one day the desire came into the sultan's heart to learn what this relic was that the nation defended with their lives and blood. The sultan burned with great passion to see what was inside the relic box. Finally he could control this desire no longer and he entered the treasury building. After all, the sentries weren't about to tell the sultan it was forbidden...The sultan, grand vizier, and viziers always freely entered the palace treasury and saw to it that the relic was in its proper place. So that's what the sultan did. After passing through forty rooms, one inside the other, the relic rested inside the forty-first room. And in that room in forty boxes, one inside the other, it was in the forty-first box.

The sultan opened the doors of forty rooms and entered the forty-first room. Then he opened forty boxes. When he held the forty-first box, his heart was beating madly in excitement. He was burning with curiosity, wondering, "What will this relic be that we have preserved all these years?"

He opened the forty-first box, looked, and what should he see: a jewel never before seen on the face of the earth. It burned like an eternal flame. If you said gold, it wasn't gold; if you said platinum, it wasn't platinum; if you said silver, it wasn't silver either. The sultan couldn't contain himself and sighed, "I'll take this holy relic left by the forebears for myself. It will be mine. How would anyone know?"

He took the holy relic—that was burning brightly like a piece torn from the sun—from its box and put it into his pocket. He put it in but was shaken by fear: "But what if it's learned that I stole it?" Then he thought: "I'll take this shiny thing and put in its place a platinum piece decorated with rubies, mother-of-pearl, emeralds, pearls, and diamonds. If one day they open the box, in view of no one's ever having seen this relic, they can't know that the holy relic was stolen."

He did as he said. Then he put the forty-first box inside each of the others, locked the forty-first and each of the other rooms, one on the other, and left the treasury. But he was terrified that the trick he had pulled would be discovered. So, though until that time they had been taking an annual oath, the sultan changed it to semi-annual so no one could know that he had stolen the holy relic. Two times each year they gathered in the square, the sultan, and others, the entire nation, and swore that they would defend the holy relic left by their forefathers with their blood and lives.

The grand vizier was a shrewd man. A suspicion came into the grand vizier's heart: "While in the old days the oath to defend the relic was taken once a year, why has the sultan changed it to twice now?" One day, saying, "What will this relic that we have preserved these many years be?" he entered the treasury. He went into the forty-one rooms, opened the forty-one boxes and saw the relic. The grand vizier was stunned when he saw this great gorgeous platinum jewel, decorated with the most precious stones, that the sultan had left in place of the relic, so his swindle wouldn't be discovered. He thought, "I'll take this relic and replace it with a gold jewel decorated with colored shiny stones. Anyway, no one knowing what the relic is, if they open the box some day they will think that is the holy relic..." He did as he said; but fearing in his heart that the trick he had pulled would be discovered, he increased the oath ceremony, which the sultan had changed to twice a year, to four times: spring, summer, fall and winter.

Unfortunately, one of the lesser viziers was a shrewd person. A suspicion entered his heart: "How come the semi-annual oath is being increased to quarterly?" Being able to enter the treasury without informing anyone, he, too, one day went in, passed through the forty-one rooms and opened the forty-one boxes. His eyes shone with pleasure when he saw the gold jewel decorated with bright stones. "I'll take this one and put silver in its place. How will anyone know?" he thought. So he did as he thought. He did it, but in his heart he had such fear that in order to hide his theft and to show the nation how well he had protected the holy relic, he started to have the quarterly oath ceremony held monthly. The populace gathered each month in the square and everyone swore to defend the holy relic to their last drop of blood.

The palace attendant was a shrewd man. He was suspicious about the oath's being changed to monthly. "There must be something up, so I'll go take a look at that relic," he said. He went through forty-one rooms, opened forty-one boxes, and saw the relic. He liked the holy relic bequeathed by the forefathers so much he thought, "If I take this and replace it with copper, how will anyone know?" And he did as he thought. He did it; but there being such fear in his heart that his theft would be discovered, in order to show the public with what fastidiousness he had protected the relic, he changed the monthly oath ceremony to weekly.

Unfortunately, the guard officer who protected the treasury was also a sly man. He said to himself, "What's going on here? We're taking the oath once a week! I'll go take a look at this holy relic..." Like the others, he too passed through forty-one rooms and opened forty-one boxes. When he saw the shiny copper he was very pleased. "I'll take this, put iron in its place, and who will know?" he said. And he did as he said. But not feeling at ease about the trick he had pulled, he started to make a big show in order to prove to everyone how hard he had tried with body and soul to defend the relic. Every day he swore that he would even take his life in his hands to protect the holy relic left by the forefathers.

Time came, time went, and a man came forth from the populace.

"Every day the entire nation swears that we will defend with our blood and lives the relic left to us by our forefathers. In truth, we preserve this relic in the treasury and defend it very well. But what is this relic? After all, we're not the custodians. Let us open these rooms and boxes and learn what this holy relic, left by our forebearers, is and why we preserve it!" he said.

These words had the effect of a bombshell. With the sultan at the head, in fear that their larceny would be discovered, all those who had committed treachery against the relic rose as one and hurled themselves at the man who had made this request. They were panic stricken that their thievery would be revealed because each one thought that only he had made this swindle by stealing the genuine relic and leaving a false one in its place. They didn't know the others had pulled the same trick.

They accused the man who had said, "Let's see what this relic is that we preserve!" of denigrating and slandering the holy relic: "Shame traitor! Who are you that you should see such a priceless, holy relic left by our forefathers!" The whole nation, fooled by them, united and fell on the man who had said this. The poor fellow was nearly lynched.

Then the sultan said, "If we're going to kill this fellow, let's do it legally!"

First a law to kill this person was written; then they executed him under the judgment of a special court.

Unfortunately, the business didn't end with his death because the words of the man who died spread from mouth to mouth. That thought gradually grew, like an avalanche. One day a citizen thought, "Why don't we take our lives in our hands and go and see what this relic is that we risk our lives to defend?" Because he knew what happened to those before him, he didn't reveal his idea to anyone. He decided to enter the treasury secretly and look at the holy relic.

But the sultan, grand vizier, and viziers, all the relic thieves, in order to hide their thefts so that no one would know, had tightened security on the holy relic left by their forefathers, more truthfully the thing they had left in its place. It was for this reason that the person who succeeded in slipping into the treasury and taking the holy relic to show to all the people, fell into the hands of the treasury guards as he emerged. In the man's hand was a rusty tin can left as a replacement by the last one to steal the relic. When the guard officer saw the can in the man's hand, he shouted:

"This is not the holy relic!"

The palace attendant said:

"That's not it!"

The vizier also said:

"That's not it!"

Then in turn all the way to the sultan they said:

"That's not it. That's not it!"

Then the man who held the rusty tin can in his hand asked:

"How do you know this isn't the holy relic? If this isn't it, what is it?"

No one there could answer this question because they all knew that the thing they left to replace the stolen relic had also been stolen later. After strangling the captured man on the spot and finishing the business, they put the rusty tin can in the box. They hid it inside the forty-one boxes and forty-one rooms. But because they were really not at ease, they passed another law for the protection of the holy relic. According to this law, morning, noon, and night, at three meals a day, the entire populace was required to take the oath that they would preserve the holy relic left by their forefathers. Not one of those who took the oath ever knew that the holy relic they preserved had been stolen and stolen until finally it had become a rusty tin can.

Aziz Nesin's wit and satiric humor have appeared in several issues of SSI. *Born in 1915 of village immigrants to Istanbul, Aziz Nesin is a prolific, international award-winning writer. He has published more than 60 books. A number of his stories have been translated into 24 languages. Joseph S. Jacobson, his gifted translator, is a university professor of languages, and a friend.*

"The evidence came to me by accident."

The Disappearance of Certain Small Communities

BY WILLIAM DOXEY

ALTHOUGH the phenomenon of vanished communities has not gone unnoticed in other parts of the United States, North Carolina historians and researchers have paid little attention to the problem. In his *History,* Holdig mentions Whitesville, but only in passing; both Dunn and Seemore ponder the mystery of Sikes, but come to no conclusions.

According to the Department of Vital Statistics' *Record,* Grant's *Register of Place-names,* and Smith Dunlap's *Gazetteer to Mid-Century,* seventy-three small communities in North Carolina have vanished. (One thousand and seven have vanished throughout the U.S.) Of this number, twenty-two disappearances were the result of "natural migration" as the early settlers pushed west. Of the remaining fifty-one, seventeen were destroyed by fire (all documented by eye-witnesses), five were leveled by tornadoes, eleven were so depopulated by the smallpox epidemic of 1833 that the survivors *en masse* were relocated and the towns totally burned, and of the other eighteen, one was destroyed by flood.

The seventeen remaining communities present a problem for several reasons. In the first place, the only evidence for their existence has been—to now—of a purely physical nature. Twelve were discovered in the course of surveys to determine legal boundaries, three were located by army personnel on maneuvers, and the other two were discovered by vacationing hikers. In many cases the physical evidence is slight, so, in fact, that in his *Cities and Towns of North Carolina* Timmons maintains nine sites are isolated farms, not communities. Be that as it may, I wish simply to note that although in recent years trained observers have explored fifteen of these seventeen locations, *no reasonable explanation for the disappearance of a single community has been given.*

The lack of all but the grossest evidence (paving stones, foundations, privy shafts, cemeteries, etc.) is unfortunate. Excepting a few firearms, plows, pots, pans, and other metal objects—all well rusted—the seventeen "unexplained" sites offer little to determine their composition. Even the cemeteries have not yielded much. Of fourteen located, not one has escaped the ravages of water erosion. Consequently, the bones have been so thoroughly mixed that no more than eleven complete skeletons (four men, three women, and four children) have been articulated.

However, there have been some positive results. Working extensively with the Granttown site, Harlow P. Clark established a population of from eighty-four to ninety-three by counting the number of spoons recovered from fourteen foundations. Even so, it would seem that we are faced with the mystery of the fate of countless individuals, unknown, who lived in nameless communities, and who passed from sight under what best can be called "strange" circumstances.

So much for background. In the remaining pages I shall present a piece of evidence of the type needed to satisfy our curiosity. It is sensational, to say the least, and might well be a hoax concocted more than a hundred years ago to cause horror and confusion in the distant future. On the other hand, in the original German it reads as the work of a highly intelligent person, one graced with an acute skill of observation and a highly developed sense of language.

This evidence came to me by accident. While researching another subject, I was exploring the storage rooms in the basement of the North Carolina Library, when I came across a large, leather-bound trunk, dusty and battered. Strangely, the librarian could find no record of the trunk in his inventory which went back to 1898. But in a ledger dated 1874 he found a note that a "Professor Parkis" had deposited a collection of "books and etc." in three trunks which he had gathered in a trip "through the mountains of western North Carolina" in 1870. The professor has been dead for many years and the two other trunks are unaccounted for.

This trunk contained a number of rolls and records from defunct banks in the west of the state. In addition, there was a small metal box approximately eleven by eight by three inches. The box was scorched. Its hinges were sprung and there was a rather deep gouge where the lid and box joined, which suggests it was found in a burned building and then forced open by the finder, who was not the owner. Inside was a diary, bound in faded red leather and cased in a green felt dust cover, which probably protected the yellowed paper from the heat of the fire.

This diary, according to the inscription on the flyleaf, belonged to a Karl Erich Stoss. The entries are written in a bold, legible hand in good German. On the first page there is a diagram which, I believe, is of the community in which Stoss lived. By comparing the drawing with the maps in Grant's *Register*, I determined it is identical with the latter's eleventh unknown community. It lies near Black Mountain, North Carolina.

I have made an inspection of the site and am convinced the two are the same. Very little remains. There is the trace of a single street which, according to Stoss, was called *"Freiheitstrasse,"* or "Liberty Street." Now an oak tree grows where wagons rolled. On either side of the street are depressions and stones which indicate foundations, on the basis of which Grant's *Register* credits the community with three stores, nine dwelling places, a smithy, a public stable, and a church-school. Stoss's diagram generally agrees, although it shows that the church-school was a *Lager*, or storehouse. On the north side of *Freiheitstrasse* are the remains of an apple orchard. The trees are hideously twisted, and what fruit I found was hard and bitter. A small stream parallels the street to the south.

Now let us consider the writer. That the diary bears his name would seem to be sufficient evidence that one Karl Erich Stoss did exist. Professor E. G. McBride tested the paper and found it to be of the same type used in the early nineteenth century. Still, to be doubly sure that the book is not a hoax, I consulted the *State Tax and Voting Rolls,* the *Lists of the Lutheran Church,* and the *Federal Immigration Record.* The *Record* states that a "Karl Erich Stoss, age 40, German of Hamburg, a blacksmith" arrived in New York City aboard the ship *Northern Cross* on April 4th, 1834. He was accompanied by his wife, Rose, age 37, and a son, Stephan, age one.

From that day in April Stoss drops from sight, not to be heard from again until the recovery of his diary, 137 years later. There is no monument to him, no stone to mark his place, for the cemetary in Freiheit (as I have come to call the community) is thoroughly eroded.

In his own writing, however, Stoss lives again, though only for a single year, if we are able to believe him, for the final entry—jumbled and confused—is dated December 14th, 1844.

From what I can determine, the events that concluded in the destruction of Freiheit and the death of all its inhabitants focus upon an individual whom Stoss refers to as the "Jackson boy." He first mentions him on March 5th:

Was to Jackson's today. He is busy about the place, as always. Karl and Fred (from other entries we learn these are Jackson's sons) at work in the barn. Saw the boy. As I rode up he was chopping wood by the kitchen. Had his shirt off. Sickly white skin was pink and blotched *(Pustel)* as though it were peeling. Strange. Weather is still cold and I was shivering in my heavy coat. But he did not mind.

Again, on March 16th, Stoss mentions him:

Jackson's boy came in today. Was barefooted and did not warm himself at my fire as other lads do. Asked for old rags. "What do you want with rags?" I asked. Said he was making something and needed them.

Stoss records that he gave him "two handfuls of dirty rags, for which I got no thanks, not even a nod." A month passes before we hear of

the boy again. It is April 15th, a beautiful spring day. Stoss says:
The air is sweet and moist and warm today. Sky clear and very
blue. No clouds. After the rain last night no wonder! Trees are
budding. Wasps are building a nest high in the eaves. Must smoke
them out. The grass is up and green. Will dig in the garden after
supper. Jackson was in today. Repaired his plow. The boy was
nowhere to be seen. To make a joke I said to Jackson, "How is the
boy's rag collection, eh?" He scratched his head and spit, and said,
"What are you talking about, Stoss?" I told him. He thought for
awhile, rubbing his ear the way both he and the boy do, and then
he said, "I may as well tell you, Stoss, because it won't be long till
all know. The boy is missing." He has run away, or perhaps been
stolen! Jackson and his sons have scouted the countryside. We
will help in the search.

And help they did, for in the next day's entry Stoss relates how a
band of seven townsmen combed the woods and hills around
Freiheit. They found nothing.

A month passed before Stoss speaks of Jackson and the boy
again. But when he returns to this subject he dwells upon it in some
detail, partly because it is in his mind, and partly because he is
bedridden with a fever and has time to think and write. On May
17th, he says:
It will soon be time to shoe Jackson's team. Jackson. I wonder
where Jackson's boy can be? He is dead? Was he stolen, or did he
run away? But why would he? Jackson is a good man. Oh, he is a
strange one, that boy! He comes from nowhere and here he is. In
Germany there are places for such as he, like the orphanage
(Waisenhaus) in Hamburg. There is something unexplainable
about that boy!

And later the same evening he returns to the subject:
I would give a dollar to know where that boy is. How can he get
away with no trail? I remember the first time I saw him. The winter
of 1837 it was, a terrible time with snow to the window ledges.
Seven years ago. My own Stephan was four. Jackson brought him
in from the forest where he found him. In the middle of winter, in
the snow! Who could do such a thing to a baby? But he was warm.
Was in an egg-shaped basket (Einform Korb) and wrapped in

thick, soft blankets. Such blankets! Like eiderdown! Ha! Wilson saw that and told Jackson maybe it was a rich man's boy and he would get a big reward. "I don't want a reward," Jackson said, "but I will take the boy, if no one comes forward to claim him." So he got him. He took him home to his farm and raised him. He was a very strange baby. Perfect. Not a wrinkle. His skin was as white as the snow they found him in, but soon with care and feeding it took on the same creamy hue as the room they kept him in. His eyes were blue and huge (kolossal). What little hair he had was so pale it seemed the same color of any object near it. Strange. The longer he lived with Jackson the more he came to resemble him. Yes! Now as I remember, when I saw him last he looked more like Jackson than Jackson's blood sons!

But apparently with the passing of the fever the thoughts of the Jackson boy pass also, for Stoss fills the pages of his diary from May 18th through the summer and autumn months to December before mentioning him again. Within this span of time, however, there are six entries which later prove to be significant. On October 1st, six months after the boy's disappearance, Stoss notes that:

Martin Weise lost a rooster and four hens last night. His dog, a splendid mastiff, is also missing. Ludlow said that maybe a vixen came after the chickens and the dog decided to get married!

But Martin Weise is not the only farmer to lose livestock. On October 22nd:

That Ludlow is not laughing now. Last night someone broke into his barn and took his sow. A chicken thief is one thing. But this? We will investigate.

But their investigation proved futile. On November 12th Stoss reports that:

It has happened again! Wilson Wright lost his milkcow. There was no moon last night. Wilson says that his dogs did not bark, but there was the sound of a strong wind, so how can he be sure? We searched for tracks and found none, *not even the cow's*. A cow does not fly, except in the nursery rime. Wilson is very sad at the loss of his cow. He has many small children who need milk. With winter coming he cannot go for another.

And winter was soon upon them. Stoss records that the first

snowfall was during the night of December 3rd:

Snow last night and early this morning. The children are delighted. I have promised to take them for a ride in the sled.

The snow brings a welcome change in routine. But on the sixth there is a minor tragedy:

Stephan is not feeling well. He played in the heavy snow today and went into the woods with James Ludlow. They said they found a nest of some kind where animals had been sleeping and had the feeling they were being watched. Grew fearful and ran all the way home, and so were overheated, then chilled. Is now in bed under blankets. Animals? It sounds like wolves, but we have seen none since the winter of '37 when the deep snow froze them out. But perhaps a pack has returned.

Stoss thinks again of wolves when, on the ninth, Wilson's cow is found:

Jackson and his sons brought in the frozen carcass (Kadaver) of Wilson's cow this noon. It is as hollow as a gourd. The skin is tight like a drum. Ludlow stood the carcass up and said "Moo!" and for a moment poor Wilson thought his cow had come to life. I searched very carefully for teeth marks. There were none, so it could not be wolves that got it. Opossums have a way of getting inside dead animals. But who—or what—stole it?

Who indeed? The question is forgotten as life proceeds normally in the small community on the tenth and eleventh. There is the expectancy of Christmas reflected in Stoss's writing. Stephan wants a rifle, which, unknown to the boy's disapproving mother, Stoss purchased along with powder and shot from a pedlar two months before. Martin Weise is chosen to supply the community Christmas tree, and, in the absence of regular clergy, Ludlow senior is elected to preach a Christmas message. Rich jars of preserves, delicious cured hams, golden canned fruits and vegetables, and stone jugs of tart cider are got together for a communal celebration, at which, says Stoss, "The good Christmas carols (Jubellieden) will be sung."

But on the twelfth of December, 1844, Karl Erich Stoss knows that there will be no Christmas. The three remaining passages are by turns lucid and incoherent. Writing the entry for the twelfth on the thirteenth, Stoss says:

They came out of the forest at noon and stood in a cluster (*Schwarm*) at the west end of the street. It was like a dream! The sun was straight overhead and bright. There were no clouds. They stood on the snow and they cast no shadows! Martin Weise's wife, Elsa, saw them first. I was in the smithy making nails when she screamed. I seized my heavy hammer and ran out. I do not know how long I stood in the snow with the hammer raised above my head. It was incredible, terrible, horrible (*schrecklich*)!

Now there is an apparent shift in time, as:

They won't break in. They want to but they won't! If only the house is strong! The shutters are frozen to the walls and I cannot lock them. But while they beat against the window-glass they do not shatter it.

And then:

They were there at the end of the street like a dream the sun the sky bright blue and they were there and no shadows and they did not sink in the soft snow they—crawl, crawl (*kriechen, kriechen*)!

Another time shift:

Ludlow's house is afire. Now Martin Weise's is also blazing. What are they doing? They—God!—they have Ludlow! They snatched him as he fled from his house. And now they have his wife and James! I can hear them! The screams (*Geschreien*)! And they say nothing. They make no sounds. But the Ludlows—and now— Oh!— the Weises are in the street. Martin has fallen and they— they have him! I must do something!

He makes an attempt to aid; however:

I could do nothing, nothing! I opened the door and shot the first one I saw. But it did no good! One of Weises's boys ran toward me. They caught him at the gate. And then they did to him what they have done to the rest. Don't you see, certain ones have long spears. They get you down and stick the spear in your chest. Then they flutter (*flatteren*) their wings and clutch you with their claws (*Klauen*). And all the while their mouths move like scissors and their huge eyes—their eyes! They are like great convex mirrors. In them you can see the whole street and the burning houses. The sun is setting. Darkness. Like a dream. I have lost a day. This is the thirteenth? Yes, it was the twelfth when they got the Powells. And the Ludlows? Twelfth? Thirteenth? I don't know. They got them, that is all that matters. I have not spoken to Rose of the ultimate consequence of this. Somehow I must sleep. Perhaps—perhaps they will go away!

But "they" do not. The entry for the fourteenth is seven pages in length and is broken chronologically in many places. The first occurrence is the appearance of Jackson, who:

> was carried through the air like a bit of straw and dropped in the middle of the street. They are not all alike. One is larger. Brighter. His body is like silver fire, like polished metal. The others obey him. He is the one who killed Jackson. The terror of it! He picked him up in his claws and pulled Jackson's head from his neck like you'd snatch a cork from a bottle. And then—then he devoured him! He put his awful mouth on the stump of Jackson's neck and when he was through, Jackson's body was as hollow as Wilson's cow!

On page three, which I judge to concern the events near noon, Stoss says:

> They brought in Jackson's sons but they did not kill them. They used the spear or stinger. And now as I look out my window—God save me!—something terrible is happening to those they stung yesterday. A grub (Raupe) is coming out of each! They have left the bodies. Each is as long as my arm. And blue against the snow. They are turning white like the snow! And now each is spinning a white, silk-like substance. What? Yes, they are making cocoons (Kokonen)! They are like the basket Jackson found the boy in!

Now it is night and all but one of the buildings in the community are on fire:

> Just before sundown they captured the Wrights. The cocoons are finished. Already the creatures have taken them away. They cradle the cocoons in their long claws and fly. At first I did not think Wilson's home would burn because of the good hardwood we used to build it. And it is snowing. They set it afire. They are patient, industrious. Strange, the fire against the snow is almost cheerful like the old times with the Christmas bonfires. They will get us tonight. One thing is clear to me. *It is the boy! The Jackson boy!* I do not know what they are. But he is the one. Before

nightfall he was at the window. He has changed, but I can tell. I know him. And he knows me! He is the one they obey. The one killed Jackson. Has always hated me! Why—why? I never spoke against him after that first time when Jackson brought him into the Smithy for warmth. He was in the basket looking up at me. A baby. But he knew! Can they hate? Those eyes! Even then. How could he have known what I said? I don't know—I can't know! Well, there is some consolation in being saved till last. My gun is loaded. They will never take us alive. It cannot be a sin—.

Here, half a page has been torn out. Stoss continues on the following sheet:

I have—killed my wife and son, my Rose and Stephan. I had to. It is dark, black with only the red of the fires and the awful white of the snow. Now it is our house afire. The end. I hear their wings, like the wind. Fanning the flames. There! The heat! It is better that we die. They want me to come out to them. To run. Never! I have my gun. I am ready! And now—with my heart too full of terror to live, I take my own life, and perish!

Thus concludes the diary of Karl Erich Stoss. The delusions of a psychopath? An attack by savage Indians? Strange animals? A new breed of insects? Alien beings? I offer no answer. Let the facts stand as they are.

There are seventeen communities in North Carolina that have disappeared; this is an eyewitness account of the destruction of one. What of the others?

Among his attributes, William Doxey has refreshing humor and a barrel of patience. He earned his PhD and is teaching at the university level, as well as working away at his short stories, poems and novels. Four novels have been published; his poems and short stories appear in many national publications.

"My wisdom came too late."

I Stand Here Ironing

BY TILLIE OLSEN

I stand here ironing, and what you asked me moves tormented back and forth with the iron.

"I wish you would manage the time to come in and talk with me about your daughter. I'm sure you can help me understand her. She's a youngster who needs help and whom I'm deeply interested in helping."

"Who needs help." . . . Even if I came, what good would it do? You think because I am her mother I have a key, or that in some way you could use me as a key? She has lived for nineteen years. There is all that life that has happened outside of me, beyond me.

And when is there time to remember, to sift, to weigh, to estimate, to total? I will start and there will be an interruption and I will have to gather it all together again. Or I will become engulfed with all I did or did not do, with what should have been and what cannot be helped.

She was a beautiful baby. The first and only one of our five that was beautiful at birth. You do not guess how new and uneasy her tenancy in her now-loveliness. You did not know her all those years she was thought homely, or see her poring over her baby pictures, making me tell her over and over how beautiful she had been—and would be, I would tell her—and was now, to the seeing eye. But the seeing eyes were few or nonexistent. Including mine.

I nursed her. They feel that's important nowadays. I nursed all the children, but with her, with all the fierce rigidity of first motherhood, I did like the books then said. Though her cries battered me to trembling and my breasts ached with swollenness, I waited till the clock decreed.

Why do I put that first? I do not even know if it matters, or if it explains anything.

She was a beautiful baby. She blew shining bubbles of sound. She loved motion, loved light, loved color and music textures. She would lie on the floor in her blue overalls patting the surface so hard in ecstasy her hands and feet would blur. She was a miracle to me, but when she was eight months old I had to leave her daytimes with the woman downstairs to whom she was no miracle at all, for I worked or looked for work and for Emily's father, who "could no longer endure" (he wrote in his good-bye note) "sharing want with us."

I was nineteen. It was the pre-relief, pre-WPA world of the depression. I would start running as soon as I got off the streetcar, running up the stairs, the place smelling sour, and awake or asleep to startle awake, when she saw me she would break into a clogged weeping that could not be comforted, a weeping I can hear yet.

After a while I found a job hashing at night so I could be with her days, and it was better. But it came to where I had to bring her to his family and leave her.

It took a long time to raise the money for her fare back. Then she got chicken pox and I had to wait longer. When she finally came, I hardly knew her, walking quick and nervous like her father, looking like her father, thin, and dressed in a shoddy red that yellowed her skin and glared at the pockmarks. All the baby loveliness gone.

She was two. Old enough for nursery school they said, and I did not know then what I know now—the fatigue of the long day, and the lacerations of group life in the kinds of nurseries that are only parking places for children.

Except that it would have made no difference if I had known. It was the only place there was. It was the only way we could be together, the only way I could hold a job.

And even without knowing, I knew. I knew the teacher that was evil because all these years it has curdled into my memory, the little boy hunched in the corner, her rasp, "why aren't you outside, because Alvin hits you? that's no reason, go out, scaredy." I knew Emily hated it even if she did not clutch and implore "don't go Mommy" like the other children, mornings.

She always had a reason why we should stay home. Momma, you look sick. Momma, I feel sick. Momma, the teachers aren't there today, they're sick. Momma, we can't go, there was a fire there last night. Momma, it's a holday today, no school, they told me.

But never a direct protest, never rebellion. I think of our others in their three-, four-year-oldness—the explosions, the tempers, the denunciations, the demands—and I feel suddenly ill. I put the iron down. What in me demanded that goodness in her? And what was the cost, the cost to her of such goodness?

The old man living in the back once said in his gentle way: "You should smile at Emily more when you look at her." What *was* in my face when I looked at her? I loved her. There were all the acts of love.

It was only with the others I remembered what he said, and it was the face of joy, and not of care or tightness or worry I turned to them—too late for Emily. She does not smile easily, let alone almost always as her brothers and sisters do. Her face is closed and sombre, but when she wants, how fluid. You must have seen it in her pantomimes, you spoke of her rare gift for comedy on the stage that rouses a laughter out of the audience so dear they applaud and applaud and do not want to let her go.

Where does it come from, that comedy? There was none of it in her when she came back to me that second time, after I had had to send her away again. She had a new daddy now to learn to love, and I think perhaps it was a better time.

Except when we left her alone nights, telling ourselves she was old enough.

"Can't you go some other time, Mommy, like tomorrow?" she

would ask. "Will it be just a little while you'll be gone? Do you promise?"

The time we came back, the front door open, the clock on the floor in the hall. She rigid awake. "It wasn't just a little while. I didn't cry. Three times I called you, just three times, and then I ran downstairs to open the door so you could come faster. The clock talked loud. I threw it away, it scared me what it talked."

She said the clock talked loud again that night I went to the hospital to have Susan. She was delirious with the fever that comes before red measles, but she was fully conscious all the week I was gone and the week after we were home when she could not come near the new baby or me.

She did not get well. She stayed skeleton thin, not wanting to eat, and night after night she had nightmares. She would call for me, and I would rouse from exhaustion to sleepily call back: "You're all right, darling, go to sleep, it's just a dream," and if she still called, in a sterner voice, "now go to sleep, Emily, there's nothing to hurt you." Twice, only twice, when I had to get up for Susan anyhow, I went in to sit with her.

Now when it is too late (as if she would let me hold and comfort her like I do the others) I get up and go to her at once at her moan or restless stirring. "Are you awake, Emily? Can I get you something?" And the answer is always the same: "No, I'm all right, go back to sleep, Mother."

They persuaded me at the clinic to send her away to a convalescent home in the country where "she can have the kind of food and care you can't manage for her, and you'll be free to concentrate on the new baby." They still send children to that place. I see pictures on the society page of sleek young women planning affairs to raise money for it, or dancing at the affairs, or decorating Easter eggs or filling Christmas stockings for the children.

They never have a picture of the children so I do not know if the girls still wear those gigantic red bows and the ravaged looks on the every other Sunday when parents can come to visit "unless otherwise notified"—as we were notified the first six weeks.

Oh it is a handsome place, green lawns and tall trees and fluted flower beds. High up on the balconies of each cottage the children stand, the girls in their red bows and white dresses, the boys in white suits and giant red ties. The parents stand below shrieking up to be heard and the children shriek down to be heard, and between them the invisible wall "Not To Be Contaminated by Parental Germs or Physical Affection."

There was a tiny girl who always stood hand in hand with Emily. Her parents never came. One visit she was gone. "They moved her to Rose Cottage" Emily shouted in explanation. "They don't like you to love anybody here."

She wrote once a week, the labored writing of a seven-year-old. "I am fine. How is the baby. If I write my letter nicely I will have a star. Love." There never was a star. We wrote every other day, letters she could never hold or keep but only hear read—once. "We simply do not have room for children to keep any personal possessions," they patiently explained when we pieced one Sunday's shrieking together to plead how much it would mean to Emily, who loved so to keep things, to be allowed to keep her letters and cards.

Each visit she looked frailer. "She isn't eating," they told us.

(They had runny eggs for breakfast or mush with lumps, Emily said later, I'd hold it in my mouth and not swallow. Nothing ever tasted good, just when they had chicken.)

It took us eight months to get her released home, and only the fact that she gained back so little of her seven lost pounds convinced the social worker.

I used to try to hold and love her after she came back, but her body would stay stiff, and after a while she'd push away. She ate little. Food sickened her, and I think much of life too. Oh she had physical lightness and brightness, twinkling by on skates, bouncing like a ball up and down up and down over the jump rope, skimming over the hill; but these were momentary.

She fretted about her appearance, thin and dark and foreign-looking at a time when every little girl was supposed to look or thought she should look a chubby blonde replica of Shirley Temple. The doorbell sometimes rang for her, but no one seemed to come and play in the house or be a best friend. Maybe because we moved so much.

There was a boy she loved painfully through two school semesters. Months later she told me how she had taken pennies from my purse to buy him candy. "Licorice was his favorite and I brought him some every day, but he still liked Jennifer better'n me. Why, Mommy?" The kind of question for which there is no answer.

School was a worry to her. She was not glib or quick in a world where glibness and quickness were easily confused with ability to learn. To her overworked and exasperated teachers she was an overconscientious "slow learner" who kept trying to catch up and was absent entirely too often.

I let her be absent, though sometimes the illness was imaginary. How different from my now-strickness about attendance with the others. I wasn't working. We had a new baby, I was home anyhow. Sometimes, after Susan grew old enough, I would keep her home from school, too, to have them all together.

Mostly Emily had asthma, and her breathing, harsh and labored, would fill the house with a curiously tranquil sound. I would bring the two old dresser mirrors and her boxes of collections to her bed. She would select beads and single earrings, bottle tops and shells, dried flowers and pebbles, old postcards and scraps, all sorts of oddments; then she and Susan would play Kingdom, setting up landscapes and furniture, peopling them with action.

Those were the only times of peaceful companionship between her and Susan. I have edged away from it, that poisonous feeling between them, that terrible balancing of hurts and needs I had to do between the two, and did so badly, those earlier years.

Oh there are conflicts between the others too, each one human, needing, demanding, hurting, taking—but only between Emily and Susan, no, Emily toward Susan that corroding resentment. It seems so obvious on the surface, yet it is not obvious. Susan, the second child, Susan, golden- and curly-haired and chubby, quick and articulate and assured, everything in appearance and manner Emily was not; Susan, not able to resist Emily's precious things, losing or sometimes clumsily breaking them; Susan telling jokes and riddles to company for applause while Emily sat silent (to say to me later: that was *my* riddle, Mother, I told it to Susan); Susan, who for all the five years' difference in age was just a year behind Emily in developing physically.

I am glad for that slow physical development that widened the difference between her and her contemporaries, though she suffered over it. She was too vulnerable for that terrible world of youthful competition, of preening and parading, of constant measuring of yourself against every other, of envy, "If I had that copper hair," "If I had that skin. . . ." She tormented herself enough about not looking like the others, there was enough of the unsureness, the having to be conscious of words before you speak, the constant caring—what are they thinking of me? without having it all magnified by the merciless physical drives.

Ronnie is calling. He is wet and I change him. It is rare there is such a cry now. That time of motherhood is almost behind me when the ear is not one's own but must always be racked and listening for the child cry, the child call. We sit for a while and I hold him, looking out over the city spread in charcoal with its soft aisles of light. *"Shoogily,"* he breathes and curls closer. I carry him back to bed, asleep. *Shoogily.* A funny word, a family word, inherited from Emily, invented by her to say: *comfort.*

In this and other ways she leaves her seal, I say aloud. And startle at my saying it. What do I mean? What did I start to gather together, to try and make coherent? I was at the terrible, growing years. War years. I do not remember them well. I was working, there were four smaller ones now, there was not time for her. She had to help be a mother, and housekeeper, and shopper. She had to set her seal. Mornings of crisis and near hysteria trying to get lunches packed, hair combed, coats and shoes found, everyone to school or Child Care on time, the baby ready for transportation. And always the paper scribbled on by a smaller one, the book looked at by Susan then mislaid, the homework not done. Running out to that huge school where she was one, she was lost, she was a drop; suffering over the unpreparedness, stammering and unsure in her classes.

There was so little time left at night after the kids were bedded down. She would struggle over books, always eating (it was in those years she developed her enormous appetite that is legendary in our family) and I would be ironing, or preparing food for the next day, or writing V-mail to Bill, or tending the baby. Sometimes, to make me laugh, or out of her despair, she would imitate happenings or types at school.

I think I said once: "Why don't you do something like this in the school amateur show?" One morning she phoned me at work, hardly understandable through the weeping: "Mother, I did it. I won, I won; they gave me first prize; they clapped and clapped and wouldn't let me go."

Now suddenly she was Somebody, and as imprisoned in her difference as she had been in anonymity.

She began to be asked to perform at other high schools, even in colleges, then at city and statewide affairs. The first one we went to, I only recognized her that first moment when thin, shy, she almost drowned herself into the curtains. Then: Was this Emily? The control, the command, the convulsing and deadly clowning, the spell, then the roaring, stamping audience, unwilling to let this rare and precious laughter out of their lives.

Afterwards: You ought to do something about her with a gift like that—but without money or knowing how, what does one do? We have left it all to her, and the gift has as often eddied inside, clogged and clotted, as been used and growing.

She is coming. She runs up the stairs two at a time with her light graceful step, and I know she is happy tonight. Whatever it was that occasioned your call did not happen today.

"Aren't you ever going to finish the ironing, Mother? Whistler painted his mother in a rocker. I'd have to paint mine standing over an ironing board." This is one of her communicative nights and she tells me everything and nothing as she fixes herself a plate of food out of the icebox.

She is so lovely. Why did you want me to come in at all? Why were you concerned? She will find her way.

She starts up the stairs to bed. "Don't get me up with the rest in the morning." "But I thought you were having midterms." "Oh, those," she comes back in, kisses me, and says quite lightly, "in a couple of years when we'll all be atom-dead they won't matter a bit."

She has said it before. She *believes* it. But because I have been dredging the past, and all that compounds a human being is so heavy and meaningful in me, I cannot endure it tonight.

I will never total it all. I will never come in to say: She was a child seldom smiled at. Her father left me before she was a year old. I had to work her first six years when there was work, or I sent her home and to his relatives. There were years she had care she hated. She was dark and thin and foreign-looking in a world where the prestige went to blondeness and curly hair and dimples, she was slow where glibness was prized. She was a child of anxious, not proud, love. We were poor and could not afford for her the soil of easy growth. I was a young mother, I was a distracted mother. There were the other children pushing up, demanding. Her younger sister seemed all that she was not. There were years she did not want me to touch her. She kept too much in herself, her life was such she had to keep too much in herself. My wisdom came too late. She has much to her and probably little will come of it. She is a child of her age, of depression, of war, of fear.

Let her be. So all that is in her will not bloom—but in how many does it? There is still enough left to live by. Only help her to know—help make it so there is cause for her to know—that she is more than this dress on the ironing board, helpless before the iron.

Tillie Olsen has won respect and reverence. A Depression high school dropout, her first book was published when she was 50. Her fame rests on a small, but gem-like body of work. Among her awards are the Ministry to Women Award from the Unitarian Women's Federation, a Doctor of Arts and Letters from the University of Nebraska and an Award in Literature from the American Academy and National Institute of Arts and Letters.

U.S. POSTAL SERVICE
STATEMENT OF OWNERSHIP, MANAGEMENT AND CIRCULATION
(Required by 39 U.S.C. 3685)

1. TITLE OF PUBLICATION	A. PUBLICATION NO.								2. DATE OF FILING
SHORT STORY INTERNATIONAL	3	7	5	9	7	0			9/22/82

3. FREQUENCY OF ISSUE	A. NO. OF ISSUES PUBLISHED ANNUALLY	B. ANNUAL SUBSCRIPTION PRICE
Bimonthly (every other month)	Six	$16.

4. COMPLETE MAILING ADDRESS OF KNOWN OFFICE OF PUBLICATION *(Street, City, County, State and ZIP Code) (Not printers)*

6 Sheffield Road, Great Neck, N.Y. 11021 (Nassau County)

5. COMPLETE MAILING ADDRESS OF THE HEADQUARTERS OR GENERAL BUSINESS OFFICES OF THE PUBLISHERS *(Not printers)*

6 Sheffield Road, Great Neck, N.Y. 11021

6. FULL NAMES AND COMPLETE MAILING ADDRESS OF PUBLISHER, EDITOR, AND MANAGING EDITOR *(This item MUST NOT be blank)*

PUBLISHER *(Name and Complete Mailing Address)*

Sam Tankel 6 Sheffield Road, Great Neck, N.Y. 11021

EDITOR *(Name and Complete Mailing Address)*

Sylvia Tankel 6 Sheffield Road, Great Neck, N.Y. 11021

MANAGING EDITOR *(Name and Complete Mailing Address)*

None

7. OWNER *(If owned by a corporation, its name and address must be stated and also immediately thereunder the names and addresses of stockholders owning or holding 1 percent or more of total amount of stock. If not owned by a corporation, the names and addresses of the individual owners must be given. If owned by a partnership or other unincorporated firm, its name and address, as well as that of each individual must be given. If the publication is published by a nonprofit organization, its name and address must be stated.) (Item must be completed)*

FULL NAME	COMPLETE MAILING ADDRESS
International Cultural Exchange (Non-profit, tax-exempt)	6 Sheffield Road, Great Neck, N.Y. 11021

8. KNOWN BONDHOLDERS, MORTGAGEES, AND OTHER SECURITY HOLDERS OWNING OR HOLDING 1 PERCENT OR MORE OF TOTAL AMOUNT OF BONDS, MORTGAGES OR OTHER SECURITIES *(If there are none, so state)*

FULL NAME	COMPLETE MAILING ADDRESS
None	

9. FOR COMPLETION BY NONPROFIT ORGANIZATIONS AUTHORIZED TO MAIL AT SPECIAL RATES *(Section 411.3, DMM only)*
The purpose, function, and nonprofit status of this organization and the exempt status for Federal income tax purposes *(Check one)*

(1) ☒ HAS NOT CHANGED DURING PRECEDING 12 MONTHS	(2) ☐ HAS CHANGED DURING PRECEDING 12 MONTHS	*(If changed, publisher must submit explanation of change with this statement.)*

10. EXTENT AND NATURE OF CIRCULATION	AVERAGE NO. COPIES EACH ISSUE DURING PRECEDING 12 MONTHS	ACTUAL NO. COPIES OF SINGLE ISSUE PUBLISHED NEAREST TO FILING DATE
A. TOTAL NO. COPIES *(Net Press Run)*	13,338	12,637
B. PAID CIRCULATION 1. SALES THROUGH DEALERS AND CARRIERS, STREET VENDORS AND COUNTER SALES	175	150
2. MAIL SUBSCRIPTION	11,050	9,548
C. TOTAL PAID CIRCULATION *(Sum of 10B1 and 10B2)*	11,225	9,698
D. FREE DISTRIBUTION BY MAIL, CARRIER OR OTHER MEANS SAMPLES, COMPLIMENTARY, AND OTHER FREE COPIES	300	300
E. TOTAL DISTRIBUTION *(Sum of C and D)*	11,525	9,998
F. COPIES NOT DISTRIBUTED 1. OFFICE USE, LEFT OVER, UNACCOUNTED, SPOILED AFTER PRINTING	1,758	2,589
2. RETURN FROM NEWS AGENTS	55	50
G. TOTAL *(Sum of E, F1 and 2 - should equal net press run shown in A)*	13,338	12,637

11. I certify that the statements made by me above are correct and complete	SIGNATURE AND TITLE OF EDITOR, PUBLISHER, BUSINESS MANAGER, OR OWNER *Sam Tankel* PUB'L

PS Form 3526

(Page 1)

The perfect gift...
for all occasions.

First gift (or your own) $16, all other gifts $14 each.

Where in the world can you find a gift like SSI? It is a gift that keeps on giving all year long, a gift that takes you to all points of the compass, to anywhere in the world. There are intriguing stories waiting for you in future issues of SSI—stories that will involve you in corners of the world you've never seen...and in worlds outside of this one...with fascinating glimpses into the future as well as the past.

Give a friend—relative—or yourself a year's subscription (6 issues) to Short Story International. The coupon below may be used for entering your own subscription and for giving a gift to impress and please. Every other month SSI will bring to you, and whomever you designate, the finest short stories gleaned from all the world—the mark of today's creative writers. Very few gifts could be more giving, more appropriate than SSI.

Order the first subscription, either your own or a gift, at the regular price of $16. Each additional subscription ordered at the same time is only $14. (This offer is good in U.S. and U.S. Possessions only and expires February 1, 1983.) Gift cards will be sent with your greetings.

A Harvest of the World's
Best Contemporary Writing Selected
and Published Every Other Month

Please enter my subscription to
Short Story International
P.O. Box 405, Great Neck, New York 11022
Six issues for $16 U.S. & U.S. Possessions
Canada $18 (US), All Other Countries $21(US).
All institutions add $2 per annual subscription.
Enclosed is my check for $_____ for _____ subscriptions.

Name _____

Address _____

City _____ State_____ Zip_____

Country _____

Please check □ New Subscription   □ Renewal

Gift for:

Name _____

Address _____

City _____ State _____ Zip _____

Country _____

Please check ▢ New Subscription ▢ Renewal

Gift for:

Name _____

Address _____

City _____ State _____ Zip _____

Country _____

Please check ▢ New Subscription ▢ Renewal

Gift for:

Name _____

Address _____

City _____ State _____ Zip _____

Country _____

Please check ▢ New Subscription ▢ Renewal

Gift for:

Name _____

Address _____

City _____ State _____ Zip _____

Country _____

Please check ▢ New Subscription ▢ Renewal

Gift for:

Name _____

Address _____

City _____ State _____ Zip _____

Country _____

Please check ▢ New Subscription ▢ Renewal

Gift for:

Name _____

Address _____

City _____ State _____ Zip _____

Country _____

Please check ▢ New Subscription ▢ Renewal

The world of the short story...
You hold the key.

The world of the short story for young people is inviting,
exciting, rich in culture and tradition of near and far corners of
the earth. You hold the key to this world...a world you can
unlock for the young in your life...and inspire in them a genuine
love for reading.

From the publisher and editor of **Short Story International,**
who for the past six years have been bringing the world's best
contemporary short fiction to you, now come two junior
editions: **Seedling Series** for elementary readers (grades 4-7),
and **Student Series** for intermediate and high school readers.

Give a Harvest of the World's Best Short Stories
Published Four Times a Year for Growing Minds.

Please enter subscription(s) to:

___ **Seedling Series: Short Story International**
     $12. U.S. & U.S. Possessions
     Canada $14 (U.S.) All Other Countries $17 (U.S.)
     All institutions add $2 per annual subscription.

___ **Student Series: Short Story International**
     $14. U.S. & U.S. Possessions
     Canada $16 (U.S.) All Other Countries $19 (U.S.)
     All institutions add $2 per annual subscription.

Mail with check to:
Short Story International
P.O. Box 405, Great Neck, NY 11022

Donor: Name _____
Address _____
City _____ State _____ Zip _____
Country _____

Send to: Name _____
Address _____
City _____ State _____ Zip _____
Country _____
Please check □ New Subscription   □ Renewal

Send to: Name _____
Address _____
City _____ State _____ Zip _____
Country _____
Please check □ New Subscription   □ Renewal
